D1431144

FIGHTING IRISH

The Summerhaven Trio #1

KATY REGNERY

Please visit my website at www.katyregnery.com

First Edition: February 2018

Katy Regnery

Fighting Irish: a novel / by Katy Regnery – 1st ed.

ISBN: 978-1-944810-27-6

To be Irish is to know that in the end, the world will break your heart.
—Daniel Patrick Moynihan

For my mother and my grandmother and all the other Irish Americans who came before me.

With kind thanks to Melissa Molloy.

xoxo

PROLOGUE

Summoned via walkie-talkie to his parents' bedroom the day before camp officially opened, fifteen-year-old Rory Haven knew what was coming, and not only did he hate this yearly ritual, but he *resented* it to the tips of his fingers and the soles of his feet.

He knew exactly what would happen.

His mother would tell her children to take a seat on the edge of her bed, and then, glowering at them, she would look each Haven triplet in the eye for a little too long, her stare searing in the vaguely terrifying, X-ray-vision sort of way that mothers around the world had perfected since the beginning of time. And when she was assured that her *trí ciarde*—or "three friends," in her native Gaelic—were sufficiently focused, she would intone in her low Killarney burr:

There'll be no fraternizin' with the guests.
Not for Rory.
Not for Ian.
Not for Tierney.
Not a lot.
Not a little.
Not at all.
Am I clear, mo thrí chairde?

This dictate was no problem for Rory's sister, Tierney,

who was a little overweight, wore thick glasses, and spoke with a slight speech impediment. She was most likely to be found by the far side of the lake reading—a.k.a. *hiding*—from the campers whose parents paid a mint for their children to attend the exclusive summer camp. Tierney would nod emphatically, relieved to have an ironclad reason *not* to mix it up with the summer guests who so intimidated her.

On the other hand, Rory's brother, Ian, with a sparkle in his emerald eyes that generally disarmed their mother, would smile at her, copying her thick brogue with a teasing wink. "Ah sure, go on, mam. Don't get yer Irish up. No fraternizin'. Okay, then."

Ian imitating their mother's accent wouldn't offend her. Most of the time, it just made her grin. But that wouldn't be the case today.

"Ian. Ah, Ian. You test me, son," she'd say, leaning down until her nose just about touched Ian's. She would grimace at him because Colleen Kelley Haven knew her children well, and she knew Ian'd be most likely to break this rule, as he had last year to disastrous results. Her brogue would be stronger for her consternation when she spoke again, the words firing at her son like so many tiny pieces of short-range shrapnel. "If ye disobey me, Ian McAllister Haven, I'll redden yer arse with a wooden spoon until ye're screamin' loud enough for t'whole camp to hear." She'd pause to let this threat sink in. "Don't think I won't. I'm not havin' another situation like last year, now." And then, because she loved Ian, she'd soften her voice just a touch, her eyes beseeching his. "Tell me you understand, son."

If Rory shot his brother a sidelong glance at that point, he'd see Ian's smile fade as his lips tightened into an angry line, his eyes flattening to a flinty green as he lowered his head in submission. "Yes, ma'am. I understand."

She'd nod crisply, as satisfied as possible, before turning to Rory.

"And you? Are you gonna be good like your sister or trouble like your brother?"

She'd wait for his answer, nailing him with a hawklike gaze as he stared back at her.

Unlike Ian, Rory was a rule-follower by nature. But unlike Tierney, he was also a people-person, excited by ideas and places far beyond their tiny world of Summerhaven.

He and his siblings lived a quiet life in Center Sandwich, New Hampshire, from September to May, where the population decreased to 123 people, only 19 of whom were under the age of 18. Heck, in their elementary school, which included kids from two neighboring villages, there were only 67 kids enrolled in the whole of grades K-6!

As a year-round resident of a summer resort area, meeting new people with fresh ideas and different experiences to share was difficult.

Except…

Except every summer, several hundred kids from affluent families in Boston, New York, Philadelphia, and all over New England came to spend a few weeks at the highly respected Summerhaven Camp for Children. Some of these campers were third-generation attendees, their grandparents proudly delivering them to a cabin that had been their own "summer haven" fifty years before. Hundreds of rich kids arrived in stylish hoards to "rough it" and "build character," bringing with them their flip-top phones, books, magazines, city ways, and slang.

And among them was one beautiful brunette with whom Rory had experienced a totally one-sided, from-a-distance love affair last summer: Brittany Manion, who was from Boston and the heiress to a hotel corporation that rivaled Marriott and Hilton.

Rory didn't care about her pedigree. Not even a little bit. He liked the way her brown eyes softened when she looked his way, the way her sweet pink lips would tilt up in a tentative smile before he forced himself to look away. He liked the way she'd wake up early to read her book on the dock, her dark hair like polished mahogany as the sun rose. He liked the way she filled out a bikini, her teenage breasts fuller than those of her friends. He liked the way her hips swelled like a woman's when so many fourteen-year-old girls still looked like boys. And he especially liked her laugh—low and soft—like she wasn't sure laughing was allowed but wasn't able to contain it.

He'd watched her endlessly last year, keeping his distance during the day while he dreamed about her every night. She was everything he wanted that he couldn't have: temptation at his fingertips—this beautiful, sophisticated girl just beyond arm's reach. And maybe, mixed with his teenage devotion to her, Rory hated her just a little bit too…because it hurt so much that he couldn't have her.

Alas. "Fraternizin'" was *strictly* forbidden. And Ian's shenanigans last year had only made their parents more exacting in the triplets' compliance.

Since Rory's great-grandfather, Truman Haven, had started the Summerhaven Camp for Children in the 1930s, every generation of Haven children had worked at the camp throughout their childhoods and adolescences, earning money and valuable work experience before leaving Center Sandwich for college.

It was well-established: Haven children weren't the guests. Haven children were, at best, management and, at worst, "the help." And with this much-despised annual ritual on the edge of her bed, Colleen Kelley Haven was reminding her three children of their place, station, rank, and responsibility.

Yes, indeed. He knew *exactly* what to expect of this annual summons.

"Hurry up, now," intoned their mother's voice over the walkie-talkie clipped to Rory's belt buckle. "I've loads of things to do today."

Rory huffed softly as he followed Ian and Tierney up the steps of the main administrative building, centrally located in the heart of Summerhaven.

On the first floor was the office where he and his parents worked year-round accepting camper applications and managing the large employee roster. For an exclusive camp the size of Summerhaven, there were grounds keepers who worked year-round in addition to tradesmen hired to fix and update camp buildings in the off-season, plus a veritable army of camp staff who were hired seasonally to run the kitchen, two dining rooms, cabin housekeeping, and laundry. Lastly, there were about twenty counsellors hired to both keep an eye on the campers and coordinate recreational and educational activities.

The office was buzzing with activity today, the day before camp officially opened, and Rory gave a lackluster wave to his father, who was on the phone, as he bypassed at the office and headed up the stairs to the Haven family apartments. Over the massive administrative building, there was a kitchen, living room, dining room, library, TV room, and three full-sized bedrooms—a huge apartment that Havens had called home for generations.

At the top of the stairs, Tierney opened the apartment door and beelined through the entry hall and living room to their parents' bedroom, ready to assure their mother than she had zero interest in making friends with the bevy of rich kids who'd be descending on them early tomorrow morning.

Following her, Ian looked at Rory over his shoulder, winking at him like he knew a secret, and Rory groaned inwardly. He knew that look, and it meant the kind of mischief that would have the wooden spoon in their mother's hand faster than you could say "Red arse."

Rory held back for a moment, watching his siblings disappear into their parents' bedroom and trying to think of a way to tell his mother that Center Sandwich was too small for him. That he loved his family—and he even loved Summerhaven—but that making friends didn't *have* to mean making trouble. He just wanted to spread his wings a little. He just wanted to know what went on in Brittany Manion's head and find out if she thought about him half as much as he thought about her. Was that really so wrong?

"Rory? Rory Kavanagh Haven, are you comin', or am I meant to come'n get you, son?"

His leaden feet moved forward, step by step over the Persian runner that covered the creaky pine floor of the hallway.

"I'm coming, Mom," he answered heavily, another wasted summer lying before him, pining for things he wanted and wishing for someone he could never have.

ChAPTER ONE

Present Day

"Mrs. Toffle, can you get Joe Schooner on the phone? The floorboards at the entrance of the south dining hall are loose again. We can't have people tripping. Can we get him in here to do a few repairs before the conference on Friday?"

"Yes, Mr. Haven," answered Miranda Toffle, who was a lifelong resident of Center Sandwich and had been working as the receptionist at Summerhaven since 1975. Without needing to consult her trusty Rolodex, she dialed Joe's number.

"And can you also call the AT&T technician? I feel like the Wi-Fi is running at half speed. I don't want any more bad reviews on Yelp."

Mrs. Toffle nodded, acknowledging Rory's second request, as she greeted Joe on the telephone and booked him for an afternoon of repairs tomorrow.

Grabbing the two ghost keys to the Oxford and Cambridge Row cottages, Rory gave Mrs. Toffle a smile of thanks then turned, tucking his clipboard under his arm as he headed out of the administrative building to check on the cottages one last time before this weekend's conference.

As he headed up the Summerhaven main path toward the lake, he passed the north dining hall and wondered—as he had thousands of times in the six years since he'd returned home to run his family's camp—*How the hell did I end up back here?*

After attending the School of Hotel Administration at Cornell University on a full scholarship, Rory had had big dreams about starting a chain of camps not wholly unlike Summerhaven in appearance but with cutting-edge conference amenities: high-speed Wi-Fi; a business center with the most updated technology for guests' use; presentation and break-out facilities; rustic-looking cottages furnished with top-of-the-line furniture, linens, and decor; gourmet food in the dining halls; a helicopter and small jet landing strip—the works. Everything a large corporation would find attractive in a place to meet for conferences, team-building weekends, global meetings, and multicompany mergers.

His business plan had won accolades from his senior-year professors, and his academic advisor had gone so far as to set Rory up with some VC, or venture capitalist, firms in New York City to start raising capital. And that's precisely where his fairytale had unhappily ended. While on the train from Ithaca to Manhattan a few weeks before graduation, Rory had received a text from Tierney.

Mom had a stroke. In intensive care at Dartmouth. Come quick.

Frozen with fear, despite the balmy May temperatures, Rory had disembarked the train in Albany, New York, rented a car, and driven to Hanover, New Hampshire, straightaway. He'd never even bothered to cancel the appointments in New York, his thoughts totally focused on the tragedy that had beset his family and hoping against hope that his mother wouldn't be gone by the time he arrived.

It turned out that Colleen Kelley Haven wasn't ready yet to "meet her maker." She survived the stroke, though it was brutal in its attack. Initially unable to breathe or swallow on her own, rehabilitation had helped greatly in these areas over the last six years. But the sad fact was that their once-vibrant mother was left mostly paralyzed on one side of her body, confined to a wheelchair, her speech slurred and her spirits low.

But the one thing that she was able to communicate clearly in the days following her stroke was that one of the Haven triplets needed to take care of Summerhaven.

Ian, who had already been in court-ordered rehab once for his all-too-frequent benders, was not a contender. From what Rory could tell from looking at him, rehab hadn't "stuck"—Ian's bloodshot eyes and gaunt face speaking volumes about how he was spending his time during his final semester at Boston University.

And while Tierney, who was about to graduate from Dartmouth, where she'd double-majored in classics and art history, was fully *capable* of running Summerhaven, Rory knew, with a triplet's intuition, that it would make her miserable. Pushing her thick glasses to the bridge of her nose, she'd looked at Rory desperately, silently begging him not to leave Summerhaven's management to her.

"I'll take care of it, Mom," Rory had said, pushing his mother's dark hair from her forehead and lowering his lips to her freckled skin. "Don't worry, yeah?"

Her eyes had closed then, and while Rory had taken some pleasure in seeing the weight of the camp fall from her shoulders, he'd suddenly felt it heavy on his own.

But then, who was better equipped than he to keep the

old place afloat? He was graduating with a bachelor's in hospitality from the best program in the country in just a few weeks. Surely he could manage Summerhaven until his mother was better and his parents were ready to take back the reins. Right? Right.

Except one summer turned into two, turned into three, turned into six.

Rory's mother was still confined to a wheelchair, though her speech was now intelligible, and she could eat unassisted. And their father, who'd pledged to stay by his wife's side "in sickness and in health," wouldn't dream of leaving Hanover, where Colleen attended physical therapy twice a week and where he was now the assistant coach for Dartmouth University soccer and baseball.

Which left Rory.

Left him, *literally*, at Summerhaven.

His walkie-talkie beeped loudly. "Go for Rory."

"Mr. Haven," said Mrs. Toffle, "can you hear me on this thing? Oh, for heaven's sake. Mr. Haven? Are you there? Over."

Sighing, he answered gently, as he always did, "Loud and clear, Mrs. Toffle."

"Oh! There you are! Joe will be in this afternoon to fix the floorboards, and AT&T is sending a technician tomorrow morning. Over."

"That's fine, Mrs. Toffle. The guests won't arrive until four or five."

"Also, you had a call. Over."

He'd mentioned to Mrs. Toffle, about a hundred times, that she didn't need to say *over* after every sentence like they were in a live-action performance of *M*A*S*H*, but she couldn't seem to break the habit.

"Can it wait?"

"Yes. She left a message. Over."

She. Hmm.

Aside from his mother and Tierney, whom Mrs. Toffle would have named, there was only one other notable "she" in Rory's life: June Thompson, a year-rounder in nearby Holderness, across the lake from Summerhaven.

"Was it June?"

How Mrs. Toffle managed to convey such stark disapproval by clearing her throat was a mystery to Rory, but nevertheless, her feelings were as clear as if she'd voiced them. "No. Over."

June, a free-spirited photographer fifteen years older than Rory who didn't care for bras and peppered her speech with more curses than a truck driver, was not a favorite of Mrs. Toffle. But June was easygoing and uncomplicated, always available when Rory wanted company without ever asking for more. They were friends *and* lovers, with no strings attached, and that suited Rory just fine.

"Take it easy on June, Mrs. T."

"Humph…over."

"So, who called?"

"Ah. Yes. A Ms. Mathison. A *lady*. Over."

Her insinuation wasn't lost on Rory, but he decided not to address it. *Mathison. Hmm.* He could only remember Mathison brothers who'd attended Summerhaven camp. *Perhaps she's a sister or cousin.*

"Did she say what she wanted?"

"Yes, she did. A venue. To get married. Over."

Rory's eyes widened and he stopped in his tracks,

letting this information sink in. He'd been trying to break into the wedding business for three years to no avail. It turned out brides didn't love the idea of a "rustic" location for their nuptials, no matter how much Rory assured them that Summerhaven was actually a rustic-themed *luxury* resort where their every whim would be met. Brides wanted posh Boston hotels or charming Upstate New York vineyards. Except…well, Miss Mathison was interested in Summerhaven. It was tremendous news.

"That's…wow! That's great, Mrs. Toffle! Did she say where she was calling from?"

"Hmmm. No. But wait! I have her number. Area code 617. Over."

Rory's fist clenched around the walkie-talkie in his hand, and he pumped it once over his head in victory. Mrs. Toffle had said 617—it was a Boston area code. *The* Boston area code. It meant that word of the Summerhaven Conference and Event Center had reached someone in Boston who wanted to have her wedding here.

Disappointment—in general, in the world—was all too familiar to Rory, and he had a sudden sinking feeling that Miss Mathison's wedding would probably be very small.

"Ummm." Rory stalled, not wanting to get his hopes up too high. "She didn't happen to mention the head count, did she?"

"Let me see. Here are my notes. Hmm. Yes!" Mrs. Toffle paused, and Rory froze, waiting for her to answer. "A minimum of two hundred and fifty people. Over."

Rory gulped. "W-Wait a m-minute, Mrs. T. Did you say two *hundred* and fifty people?"

"I did. Over."

"*Holy shit!*" he bellowed. "*Yes!* Yes yes yes yes yes!"

Rory jumped up and down on the main path like a maniac, pumping his hand in the air as he did the math quickly in his head. If this was a destination wedding for at least one hundred of those guests planning to stay overnight—in addition to catering, activities, and decorations—he was looking at a very tidy profit. Maybe even enough money to hire someone *else* to take care of Summerhaven this summer while Rory Kavanagh Haven, after years of dutifully waiting, spent a few months raising funds for the business plan he'd been sitting on for six years.

"Mr. Haven?" asked Mrs. Toffle, her New England accent extra salty. "Are you finished cursing? Over."

Chagrined, Rory stifled a chuckle. "Yes, ma'am."

"She was hoping to visit on Friday. I told her you'd call her back today. Over."

"Mrs. Toffle," said Rory, "will you do me a favor? Call her back right away and make an appointment. Anytime before four o'clock. And Mrs. T? Pray this works out, huh?"

She laughed good-naturedly over the walkie-talkie, then added with a bit of sass, "You don't need my prayers, Rory Haven. I've heard you with potential clients. You could charm the pants off the devil."

He grinned, imagining her red cheeks at such a bold admission and realizing an excellent opportunity to tease her when it landed on his doorstep. "Why, Mrs. Toffle—"

"Save it for Ms. Mathison, Mr. Haven," she advised sagely, then added for good measure, "Over and out."

chapter two

Brittany Manion Mathison was feeling victorious.

After a six-month engagement, last night over dinner, her fiancé, Benjamin Parker, MD, had *grudgingly* consented to a Memorial Day weekend wedding. Yes, it had taken a covert mission to his office, where she'd tricked his receptionist into combing his schedule for a free weekend when he wasn't on call, but once she'd presented Ben with the date, it was nothing short of a fait accompli: he'd been unable to argue with her.

And while it was true that a late-May wedding meant that Brittany only had seven weeks to plan, she refused to be daunted. In fact, she'd already pictured the perfect place to get married and already made an appointment to visit.

"I hope I can get everything done in time," said Brittany as she stared at the date, circled in red ink, in her day planner.

"Keep it simple," advised Ben, combing his hair in the mirror over her bureau. "Just choose a place and send out a save-the-date. How difficult can it be?"

"To throw together a wedding in seven weeks? Are you kidding?" she replied, looking at him incredulously from where she was still lying in bed. She scoffed softly. "And send an e-mail? No. Absolutely not. That's not *done*. My mother would die."

"Well, if anyone can throw it together, you can," he said, glancing at her over his shoulder. "In fact, why don't you take a break from your charities and concentrate on this for a few weeks? You'll get everything done. Planning things quickly is your secret superpower."

It was a cute compliment and softened her annoyance at his suggestion that she "take a break" from her "charities," like founding and running a nonprofit was an indulgence, not real work.

While most of her peers worked at conventional jobs, Brittany, whose trust fund ensured that she didn't require an additional income, had set up a successful foundation in the years following her college graduation, and she took its management and growth as seriously as any paying job. More, even. Her nonprofit, A Better Tomorrow, which helped recovering addicts get their lives back on track, was born of her heart, and she'd put her wallet and her soul into its success.

But Ben was probably right. If Brittany cut back her hours and put her responsibilities as board chairwoman of A Better Tomorrow in the hands of her capable staff from now until Memorial Day, she might be able to get everything done in time.

"Hmm. I'll think about it. Maria and Joy could probably take care of things if I took a leave." She looked up at Ben, catching his eyes in the mirror before he looked away. He hadn't been over the moon about her fait accompli last night. "You're excited, aren't you? To get married?"

Dressed in jeans and a T-shirt, Ben would change into scrubs when he got to Mass General, where he was an emergency room pediatrician. He looked at her again like he wanted to say something, but instead he took a deep breath and sighed.

"Sure I am. There's just—I mean, there's no reason to go nuts planning, right? In fact, since this will be a second wedding for both of us, let's just keep it simple, huh?"

She tried to ignore the disappointment that washed over her at his lackluster response, but then again, maybe he was right.

Ben, who was fifteen years her senior at forty-two, had married right out of med school to a fellow pediatrician. They'd had two daughters, one who was about to graduate high school while the other was finishing eighth grade. And frankly, neither had seemed very thrilled when their father had announced his engagement to Brittany at Thanksgiving, nor very receptive to her overtures at friendship over the past few months.

"Will the girls attend?" she asked softly, hating how much she wanted them to be there, how much she wanted for them—her and Ben—to be a family.

He turned to look at her, offering a small, conciliatory smile. "Of course they will."

She huffed softly, picking at the embroidered quilt on her lap. "I think Angela's poisoned the well."

Angela, Ben's ex-wife who still worked in the pediatric department at Mass General, saw Brittany as an interloper, even though she and Ben hadn't even met until a year after his divorce was final. Brittany could tell by the way Ben's daughters looked at her: their mother, who was still single two years after the divorce, was not on board with her husband's new fiancée.

"That's not true," said Ben, his voice warming as he jumped to Angela's defense, as he always did. "Listen, Angie's just…she's a good person, baby. She was—you know, she was hurt by—by the divorce."

I'd be hurt too, thought Brittany, *if you'd cheated on me.*

She immediately counterbalanced that unkind thought with a stronger, better one: *That won't happen to us. I intend to stay home with our children, not work long hours at a hospital. I won't give you any reason to stray.*

"I need you to try to understand," said Ben gently, sitting on the edge of the bed beside her and taking her hands in his. "Angie's *always* going to be a part of my life. Without her, I wouldn't have Gracie and Sabrina. I'm grateful to her for giving me those amazing girls, and she's— she's a wonderful mother, Brittany. You can see that, right? I really need for all of you to get along."

He reached up to cup her cheek and Brittany closed her eyes, nestling against his warm palm. "I'll try harder, Ben. I promise."

"That's my girl."

She opened her eyes and looked up at him—at his strong features, bright-blue eyes, and dignified salt-and-pepper hair. "You're crazy handsome."

"And you're crazy beautiful."

Her heart lurched with tenderness, a question she wanted to ask on the tip of her tongue, but she didn't want to press her luck. He'd finally consented to a date after putting it off for six months. She needed to count her blessings and enjoy that major development. She'd wait for another moment to address the matter weighing on her heart.

"Love me?" she asked instead.

"You're Brittany Manion," he answered, leaning forward to kiss her forehead. "How could I not?"

"I love you too," she said. "Tons."

He grinned at her, grabbing his keys from the bedside table and tucking them into his pocket as he stood up. "I'm working a double today and tomorrow, and then I'm having the girls over at my place on Sunday for an overnight. See you on Monday? Maybe for dinner at Romolo's?"

"Maybe I could come over and cook on Sunday?" she asked hopefully. "Spend some time with you and the gi—"

"Baby, don't take this the wrong way, but I want to talk to them alone about the wedding date, okay? I think it'll go better if it's just me and them."

"Oh. Right," she said, feeling deflated. "Of course."

She sighed. Not only did another long weekend lie before her without Ben's company, but how was she supposed to make inroads with his daughters if he didn't encourage them all to spend time together?

"I'm trying to do what's best for everyone, Brittany," he said, his voice taking on a slight edge.

"I know," she said, offering him a brave smile.

Don't be selfish, the voice in her head whispered. *He's working a double shift to save lives. Babies' lives. And he's a great dad to those girls. The sort of dad you want your own children to have.* Her heart contracted at the sweetness of the thought.

"You're a good man, Ben Parker."

"I do my best," he answered, leaning down to kiss her forehead again.

Do you? asked the voice in her head. *Were you doing your best when you cheated on Angela? Would you ever walk out of this room after kissing me sweetly and cheat on me?*

Disappointed in the disloyalty of her thoughts, she stifled them instantly, throwing a bucket of water over the nagging embers. "You *are* the best."

And you'll be the best dad ever.

"You'll give me a big head if you keep saying things like that," he said, winking at her as he left the bedroom. "Have a great weekend, beautiful," he called over his shoulder, his footsteps receding softly down the hall to the front door of her apartment.

The best dad ever.

That was worth any challenges offered up by the Parker women, worth any low-grade uncertainties she had that were, most likely, a product of her *own* insecurities, not Ben's long-ago, one-time indiscretion. He would be an *amazing* father. And for Brittany, who wanted children of her own more than anything else on earth, that fact alone made Ben the perfect match for her.

As the only child of hotel magnate Phillip Manion and his wife, Charlene, Brittany had wanted for very little in her life, materially speaking. She had lavish bedrooms in each of her parent's houses, nannies and maids to see to her every need, playrooms that looked like mini FAO Schwartz stores, and closets-full of the most expensive, beautiful clothes in the world.

She was sent to the most exclusive boarding schools and summer camps, to Broadway premieres on her father's private jet, to parties in Paris on a whim. She spent summers in Tuscany and Christmases in Aspen. She was the very definition of privileged, and she was very grateful for such a comfortable upbringing.

But at the same time, she mourned the fact that she'd had no siblings with whom to share her decadent, wildly lonely childhood. Especially after her parent's divorce, she'd felt very alone in the world, shuttled from house to house and school to camp, a kind nanny or companion no substitute for someone who loved you, who truly *belonged* to you.

Brittany Manion, poor little rich girl, knew what it was to feel fiercely, savagely, and brutally lonesome, and at some point, she'd decided that there was only one thing that could assuage the longing in her soul and fill the hole in her heart: a child of her own. Someone related to her, who belonged to her, to whom she belonged. And then, finally—*finally*—Brittany wouldn't be alone anymore.

When she'd married Travis Mathison, whom she'd known since childhood, she was sure she'd made the right choice. The youngest of six siblings, Travis was close to his family and a doting uncle to his nieces and nephews. The problem? He didn't want children of his own. Not yet, anyway. He liked them well enough, but Travis was young and wanted to party; fatherhood wasn't on his radar. "Not yet, Brittany," he'd been fond of saying. "Don't rush me. Not yet."

After three years of marriage, they'd amicably divorced.

And last year, on New Year's Eve, Brittany had seen a picture on Facebook of Travis, his new wife, and their almost one-year-old son.

Tears ran down her face as she'd stared at the picture, wondering what was wrong with *her*, why Travis had refused to have children with her but had fathered a son with someone else a couple of years later. Why didn't anyone want to be *her* family? What was she doing *wrong*?

She'd gone out for cocktails with her friend Hallie that evening and asked Ben Parker the same question when she'd found herself sitting next to him at a bar after way too many martinis.

He'd cupped her cheeks and kissed her gently, smiling at her tenderly before whispering in her ear, "Nothing, beautiful. You're not doing anything wrong. And I bet your babies will look like angels someday."

And just like that, her tears had stopped, and her heart had started beating for Ben. And when she found out he was a single pediatrician, devoted to his two daughters? It felt like God's hand on her life. Things hadn't worked out with Travis, but now she saw the bigger picture: all roads had led her to Ben. And with Ben was *exactly* where she was supposed to be.

Sighing with a renewed sense of purpose, Brittany swung out of bed and padded across the plush carpet of her bedroom to the en suite bathroom. Looking at herself in the mirror, she grinned. "No more brooding. You have a wedding to start planning today."

Pulling her nightgown over her head, she dropped it on the floor, then opened the shower door and turned on the hot water.

She had a noon appointment with Mr. Haven at the Summerhaven camp in New Hampshire, where she'd spent four happy summers as a girl. And she didn't want to be late.

Two hours later, Brittany crossed over the Massachusetts

border into New Hampshire, rolling down her window so the early spring sun could warm her arm as she belted out the words to "Heart of Mine" by Peter Sallett.

"*There's always something so tragic…about a hopeless romantic!*" she sang, grinning out the windshield of her silver Aston Martin One-77, a completely over-the-top purchase she'd made from her trust fund two years ago. At a cool $1.7 million, it was the most expensive car she'd ever owned, but it was sheer heaven to drive, and she couldn't help sighing with pleasure as she shifted into fifth gear.

Brittany wasn't given to extravagant purchases of this magnitude on a regular basis, but something about the beautiful little sports car—perhaps the fact that Travis had hated the whole Aston Martin brand, calling it "pretentious, British bullshit"—made it a must-have for her in the months after her divorce. And, she reasoned, it was so well made, so infrequently used, and one of two hundred ever made, it would only appreciate as an investment. Besides, as a 12 percent shareholder of Manion International Hotels, Brittany really didn't need to worry about her spending habits. Her trust fund would keep her solvent for the next three hundred years no matter how many Aston Martins filled her garages.

Her phone, in the center console, buzzed with an incoming call, and Brittany pressed the Bluetooth button, which faded out her song.

"Hello?"

"Miss Mathison?"

"This is she. Mr. Haven?"

"Yes. Just checking in."

"I'm on my way. Should be there on time for our appointment," she said, wondering how much Mr. Haven had changed over the past decade since she was last at Summerhaven.

The Haven family, who owned and ran the camp, had seemed omnipresent at Summerhaven—everywhere and yet nowhere at the same time. They would be in the dining room when meals began but slip out as the campers took their assigned seats. They would drive a van of campers to the local historic center but wait outside in the parking lot while the campers took a tour. They would slip out of a cabin holding an armful of dirty linens and disappear down an unmarked path that led to the laundry. Mostly, they blended in, as much a part of the camp as the woods or the lake, intrinsic to the experience itself.

Except…

Except Rory.

Rory Haven wouldn't really "blend in" anywhere.

Brittany remembered how hard her heart would flutter when she caught sight of handsome Rory. She couldn't ever remember him smiling at her, but that hadn't kept her from developing a wild crush on him for four consecutive summers, always vying for a glimpse of him and savoring the infrequent moments when she could quietly observe him.

He had felt utterly off-limits to her, which only added to his allure. With muscles that none of her own peers boasted, cheeks carved from marble, and shaggy dark-brown hair that flopped sinfully over his forehead to cover his emerald eyes, she had often wondered, in later years, if she'd dreamed him or embellished him. He couldn't have possibly been *that* beautiful, could he?

Sighing over her memories, she shifted her thoughts back to Rory's father, Mr. Haven, remembering his warm, friendly smile and how he'd gently admonish the teenage girls when they'd gotten into mischief. His wife, Mrs. Haven, on the other hand, was a holy terror with a razor-sharp tongue who had no problem sending wayward children back to their parents if they didn't behave at Summerhaven. You didn't want to get on *her* bad side, but Mr. Haven? Brittany remembered him as a big bearded teddy bear, and she looked forward to renewing his acquaintance now, as an adult woman, and thanking him for his hospitality over several memorable summers.

Pushing her recollections aside, she tuned back into their conversation.

"…would be nice," Mr. Haven was saying, "if you'd join me for lunch. We have a large group coming in this afternoon around four o'clock, and the smells coming out of the kitchen are…well, frankly, mouth-watering."

"Oh." She hesitated a moment, wondering if Mrs. Haven, with her inscrutable, hawklike stare, would be joining them too. "Um, I hadn't planned on—"

"It really would be a great opportunity for you to test out Chef Jamie's skills," he added.

"Will Mrs. Haven be joining us as well?"

"Mrs.—oh, um, no." He paused for a moment, then added, "There is no Mrs. Haven."

"Oh, dear," she said, cringing at this news. Poor Mr. Haven. Despite his wife's cool disposition, Brittany had seen them walking down the main path in the evening, hand in hand, more than once. He had always seemed genuinely fond of her, and Brittany imagined her passing had been very painful for him. "I'm so sorry."

Mr. Haven chuckled softly. "Well, I'm not ruling out a

Mrs. Haven…someday."

Well, you've gotten over the loss of your first wife mighty fast, she thought, feeling a little bit disappointed in Mr. Haven, and in herself, for misjudging their devotion to one another.

"So…lunch?" he asked.

Brittany reminded herself that Mr. Haven's marital status, or lack thereof, wasn't her concern, and her stomach growled to let her know that his invitation was both timely and welcome.

"Right. Well, sure. Yes. Lunch sounds lovely. Thank you. Any chance Chef Jamie is whipping up a wedding cake I can sample?" she joked.

"No, I'm afraid not. But if you do end up booking your event with us, we'll have you and your fiancé back up for a complete tasting based on your preferences and choices."

"Thank you."

"Of course. We aim to offer complete luxury in a rustic setting. Drive safely. See you soon, Miss Mathison."

Ms., she thought, though she didn't correct his innocent mistake. However, she did remind herself—for the hundredth time—that she needed to send in the paperwork to have Mathison dropped from her legal name so she could officially be Brittany Manion Parker in the very near future.

"See you soon, Mr. Haven."

The line went quiet, and a moment later Peter Sallett's voice filled the car again with the words, *I'm through with waiting…and hesitating. I want you taking this heart…of…mine.*

And Brittany stepped on the gas, ever closer to the place of her best memories that would host the wedding of her dreams.

chapter three

Rory hung up the phone, then grimaced. "Shit!"

He'd forgotten to ask Miss Mathison how she'd heard about Summerhaven. Oh, well. He'd be certain to ask her when she arrived. No doubt he owed an ex-camper a debt of gratitude for mentioning it to her, and Havens paid their debts.

He grinned as he walked back toward the dining room to prepare a table for their luncheon. He didn't know how old she was, but he'd bet she was over forty. She seemed very formal, calling him Mr. Haven in her cultured, but almost obsolete, Brahmin accent.

He'd heard that accent enough in his childhood to know it meant money.

Hmm, he thought, swinging open the door to the dining room, *maybe I should Google her before she arrives and see if she's someone who should already be on my radar?*

He'd barely had a free moment to do anything but prepare for this weekend's conference, but he *was* free for a little while before she arrived. Taking out his phone, he tapped on the Chrome app just as it rang.

Tierney.

"Tierney? What's up?"

She sighed, long and hard. "Ian. That's what."

"*Shiiiite*," he murmured, their mother's favorite curse word coming back effortlessly, as it always did when he was speaking with his brother or sister. "Tell me."

"He showed up at my place last night. After midnight. Scared me to death banging on the back door of the cottage."

Warring feelings of relief and anger flooded Rory. He was glad that his brother had finally turned up, but not too thrilled that he'd terrified Tierney by waking her up in the middle of the night.

"Where the hell's he been since November?"

"Who knows?" she said. "He was barely coherent when he got here. An Uber dropped him off and I had to help him inside. He's still sleeping it off in the guest room."

Rory didn't need to ask what "it" was. Ian's drinking habits since college had only worsened. Over the last six years, he'd spent two more stints in rehab and been arrested several times in Boston for drunken disorderly conduct. And last fall, he'd finally lost his job as a high school ice hockey coach after showing up intoxicated to a game and shoving a ref. Soon after, he'd become homeless, and since then, it had been incoherent, rambling voice mail messages on his and Tierney's phones, with very little rhyme or reason.

"Did you go through his bag?"

"Of course."

"And?"

"Half a full-sized bottle of vodka and a bunch of airplane-sized bottles of—"

"Doesn't matter."

"I poured it all down the sink."

"Good girl." He took a deep breath and ran his fingers

through his hair. "What have you got there?"

"You know me better than that," said his sister. "Even the cough syrup I had went to the dump this morning."

Rory nodded. Both he and Tierney knew the drill. Ian had even been known to drink red wine vinegar when he was desperate. It all had to go in the trash the moment he landed at one of their homes.

Rory looked at his watch. Miss Mathison would be here in about forty-five minutes, but Tierney only lived ten minutes away, in the caretaker's cottage at Moonstone Manor, a historic landmark in neighboring Moultonborough, New Hampshire. She was the caretaker and curator of the estate museum, which was located on five thousand semi-isolated acres owned by the state.

"Need me to come over?"

"Yes," she said without hesitation. "But not right this minute. He's dead to the world. Later. When he's up. How about six? You could bring dinner?"

Tonight wasn't terrific, frankly. Forty conference attendees would be arriving between four and five o'clock, and Rory needed to be at Summerhaven to greet them and help settle them in.

But family came first for the Haven triplets. Always had. Always would. No matter what.

"Can we make it seven, Tier? I have a group coming in—"

"*Damnú*," she cursed in Gaelic. "I forgot about that! I can handle Ian. Don't worry about—"

"Stop. I'll be there at seven. I promise."

"Okay then, Rory. *Tá grá agam ort.*"

"Love you too," he answered, ending the call before

shoving his phone in the back pocket of his jeans with a long sigh. "*Damnú*, Ian."

When was this going to stop? When would Ian finally get well? Get his life back on track? Make something of himself? Rory loved Ian—loved his brother like his own arm or leg or heart. But loving someone as destructive as Ian was exhausting.

But there would be enough time to focus on Ian when he got to Tierney's place tonight. For now, he needed to set an elegant table for Miss Mathison and put his best foot forward. If he didn't, he could kiss his *own* dreams farewell.

Brittany turned into the parking lot marked "Visitors," enjoying the crunch of her wheels over the uneven dirt and pebbles. Exiting her car, she raised her arms over her head and stretched, shrugging out of her red cashmere cardigan and tying it around her waist.

Underneath, she wore a pair of Balmain skinny jeans, and on top, a Brooks Brothers button-down shirt in dress Stewart plaid. Traditional Bass penny loafers without socks rounded out her preppy outfit. Reaching back, she gathered her honey-blonde hair at the base of her neck and wound it into a loose bun, then reached back into the car for her purse and slung it over her shoulder.

"Please Check In at the Office" advised a dark-brown sign with bright white letters and an arrow pointing to the large administrative building that Brittany recognized.

Breathing deeply, she grinned as she walked from the parking lot to the main office. Despite the fact that the sign outside the camp now read "Summerhaven Conference and Event Center" instead of "Summerhaven Camp for Children," as it used to, it still smelled the same. Fir trees and fresh air, the lumber used to build the cabins, and the leftover smoke from a thousand magical campfires—it made Brittany inexplicably happy.

As she pulled open the screen door to the office, it squeaked cheerfully on decades-old hinges, conjuring more happy memories. Awash in nostalgia, Brittany smiled at the white-haired receptionist who looked up from her desk.

"Hi, there," she said. "I'm—"

"Brittany Mathison, I should think," said the older woman, standing up and extending her hand over the polished pine counter. "I'm Miranda Toffle. We spoke on the phone."

"Of course! I remember you, Mrs. Toffle! You were here when I was a camper."

"Hold on, now. Were you a camper here, dear?"

"Yes," said Brittany, squeezing Mrs. Toffle's hand once more before letting it go. "For four years when I was a teenager."

"And here I thought I had an elephant's memory. I don't remember any Mathison girl camping here. Just a family of, uh, six brothers who came up for a few years. Hmm. Wait, now. Was it five or—? Nope. Six. It was six. I'm sure of it."

"So am I," said Brittany, leaning forward just a little and lowering her voice conspiratorially. "I was married to one of them."

"You don't say!"

"I do," she said, giggling softly at Mrs. Toffle's

surprised face. "My maiden name was Manion."

"Oh!" Mrs. Toffle gasped. "Manion. Brittany Manion! Of course! You were here for—let me see—2004 through 2007, right?"

"Exactly right! My goodness, you *do* have an elephant's memory!"

"I pride myself on it," said Mrs. Toffle. "Welcome back to Summerhaven, Brittany Manion!"

"It's changed."

"From a camp to a conference center? My, land! Yes."

"Do you mind my asking why?"

"I suppose Mr. Haven could answer you better than I," said Mrs. Toffle, gracefully sidestepping an explanation. "Speaking of…he said that you should be directed to the north dining room when you get here. Do you remember how to…?"

"Down the main path about a tenth of a mile, and it'll be down the hill on the right."

"Now who's the elephant?" asked Mrs. Toffle with a twinkle in her eye.

Brittany chuckled softly. "Should I check in again before I leave?"

"No need," she said, turning to sit back down at her desk. "I expect Mr. Haven will walk you back to your car."

"Well, then, I'll just…" She gestured loosely to the door with her sunglasses as Mrs. Toffle sat back down at her desk, feeding a piece of crisp white paper into an old typewriter.

Turning away, Brittany let herself back out of the office door and hopped down the steps that led to the path. It was a bright, warm April day, and as she walked, she remembered the first time her father had dropped her off at

Summerhaven.

"But Daddy, I don't want to stay here," she'd lamented, sitting beside him in the backseat of their Rolls Royce. "Please let me go to Paris with you. I won't be a bit of trouble."

"I came to Summerhaven when I was fourteen and had the time of my life. So will you."

"But I don't know anyone here."

"Nonsense! Chet Mathison sends his sons here."

"The Mathison boys are hellions."

"Humph." He grumbled softly. "Well, I believe Kip Holt sends his girls here too. You know them, don't you?"

Missy, Kitty, and Posy Holt? Sure, they took tennis lessons together. A chill went down her spine, but she didn't say any more. Her father disliked expressions of weakness. Telling him that she was completely and totally terrified of the Holt sisters wouldn't do anything except raise his ire.

"Yes, Daddy."

"There it is, then. People you know."

She'd been scared. Oh, Lord, she'd been so scared after he'd dropped her off and one of the counsellors from the main office had walked her to her cabin, which was named "Lady Margaret" after one of the colleges at Oxford University.

But it turned out that her fears were unfounded and unnecessary.

First of all, the Holt sisters already had their circle of friends at Summerhaven and had mostly ignored Brittany.

Second of all, the Mathison boys in attendance— Archie, Jasper, and Travis—had been kind to her whenever she ran into them.

And third of all, her bunkmates—Hallie from Boston, Chelsea from Greenwich, and Tate from Quogue—were all first-time attendees like Brittany, who'd been called "Britt" at Summerhaven, though never before or since. They became fast friends over that summer, and Lady Margaret rang with their laughter for three years following.

While Brittany still saw Hallie in Boston from time to time, she'd lost touch with Chelsea and Tate over the years. Maybe, she mused, turning right down the path that led to the lakeside north dining hall, she should look them up. Being back at Summerhaven even for a few minutes was already making her miss them.

Glancing ahead, she realized that the old dining hall had been modernized. Yes, it still fit in with the unfinished pine, New England camp-style architecture that defined Summerhaven, but if one looked closely, you could easily tell that it was far more modern. Gone was the mossy roof and crumbling stone chimney of yore. The building before her now was stunning.

"Miss Mathison?"

Her gaze slid from the shiny copper roof to find a man propping open the dining room door. Even backlit by the sun as he was, she could see that he was young, tall, and muscular—not at all the way she remembered old Mr. Haven.

Drawing her sunglasses from her eyes to the top of her head, she stepped forward into the shade and looked up again—straight into the dazzling green eyes of Rory Haven.

Miss Mathison blinked at him, gasped, and then blinked again.

"Miss Mathison?" he repeated, scanning her face for signs of distress. "Are you well?"

"You're not Mr. Haven," she whispered.

"Yes, I am. I'm Rory Haven," he said, tucking his clipboard under his arm and offering her his hand. "Welcome to Summerhaven."

"Rory," she said, nodding at him as her pink lips spread into a grin. "Thank you."

Looking up at him, with her warm-brown eyes locked on his, he suddenly got the feeling that he'd met her before, but he couldn't place where. They hadn't had any female campers named Mathison. Perhaps she was a sister of the Mathison brothers and had come for Family Day one year? Or for drop-off weekend? She was too lovely to forget.

"Do we know each other?" he blurted out.

"Not really," she said mysteriously, stepping forward through the dining room door that he still held open.

Following her inside and letting the door slam shut behind him, he waited for her to turn around and face him. When she did, he was struck by the feeling of familiarity again, only it was ten times stronger now that he could see her clearly. He *knew* this woman. They'd definitely met before.

"You look *really* familiar," he said.

"I thought I was meeting your father for lunch," she said, reaching up for her sunglasses. She pulled them from her head, folded them closed, and slipped them into the leather bag on her shoulder.

"Do you *know* my father?"

"I've met him, yes. Several times."

"When? You couldn't have been a camper here. I would have remembered your name, but—"

"But there were only Mathison brothers at Summerhaven," she said with a little chuckle. She gestured to a small table, covered with a white tablecloth, that Rory had set up by the windows. "Is that for us?"

"Uh…yes. But not until you tell me how I know you, or it'll drive me nuts."

She turned and bent her head back to look up at him, her brown eyes mischievous and merry. "I was a camper here. For four summers. A long time ago."

Rory shook his head. "No. I would have remembered you."

"You *do* remember me," she said, weaving through the other tables in the dining room to get to theirs. "You just don't recognize me by my married name."

"Your…married name."

"Uh-huh."

"Forgive me, but aren't you here to—"

"Get married? Yes. My ex-husband is Travis Mathison," she clarified, standing beside the table.

Rory pulled out her chair, waited until she sat down, then pushed it in and rounded the table to take his own seat, still staring at her smiling face with growing impatience. Who was she? Who was she?

Who are you?

Although he had been forbidden to socialize with the campers, he'd had his favorites, of course. During high school, in particular, he'd especially liked this group of four girls who'd stayed in Lady Margaret, one of the ten Oxford

Row cabins for girls. In fact, he thought, taking his seat and regarding her across the table, Miss—well, Ms.—Mathison was a dead ringer for...

Oh my God.

"Brittany Manion."

She nodded, giggling softly as she reached for her white linen napkin and spread it across her lap. "Bingo."

"But you were a brunette."

"And you were five foot two."

He chuckled along with her. "Fair enough."

"You married Travis Mathison?"

"I did," she answered, nodding at Rory.

"Welcome to Summerhaven, Miss Mathison," said Victor, the head waiter that Rory always hired for upscale luncheons and dinners at the conference center. "Tap or sparkling?"

"Tap is fine. Thank you."

He cleared his throat, then recited from memory, "Lunch will be a salad of in-season greens, avocado slices, and grapefruit sections, followed by grilled salmon with a hollandaise sauce."

"How lovely."

"May I bring you a glass of Pinot Grigio?"

"Sanctioned alcohol at Summerhaven?" she asked, shifting her gaze to Rory with a minxy grin. "Things certainly *have* changed." Leaning forward, she asked, "Are you drinking?"

The correct answer was no. Rory wasn't much of a drinker anyway, but with a big group coming in later, he needed to be on his game. He didn't look away from Brittany as he answered, "Yes. Sure. I'd love a glass, Victor."

"Me too, Victor," said Brittany, grinning up at the older man. When she looked back at Rory, she was still smiling. "What?"

"I'm staring," said Rory, "aren't I?"

"You're staring."

He looked down, reaching for his napkin and placing it on his lap to distract himself. Brittany Manion. Beautiful, rich, kind, sweet Brittany Manion. How many years had it been since Rory had thought of her? Ten, at least.

If he'd been allowed to talk to the guests, to date the guests, to choose one guest to dance with at the season-end square dance every year, it would have been Brittany Manion, no question.

A decade had only heightened her beauty—she was petite, no more than the five foot two she'd just kidded him about. But her eyes were still the same warm brown that had tortured him from a distance when he thought she wasn't looking, and the wisps of her now blonde hair escaping from her bun only emphasized her classic Grace Kelly features.

She was, hands down, the loveliest woman he'd ever seen, then as now…

…and so far out of his league now, as then, that moving beyond admiration didn't even occur to him.

She was Brittany Manion of the Boston Manions.

And besides, she was here to get married.

Chapter Four

"So much has changed in ten years," she said, trying to make polite conversation and alleviate a bit of the tension between them.

To say she'd been stunned by Rory Haven's sudden appearance would be an understatement. It hadn't even occurred to her that the camp once run by his parents would now be managed by him—by the dark-haired, brooding boy she'd crushed on as a teen. And what a man he'd turned into.

A little over six feet tall with pecs that popped, just a touch, behind his Summerhaven polo shirt and a jawline cut from marble, Rory was mouth-watering now.

She reached for her water glass, taking a long sip while he answered her.

"Uh, yes. I took over management from my parents six years ago."

She nodded, hoping that he'd tell her a little more.

"Several years ago, my mother had a stroke," he explained.

Brittany gasped, feeling bad for every unkind thought she'd had about Mrs. Haven on her drive north. "I'm so sorry, Rory."

"She's still alive."

"Oh, good."

"But she's not the same. She's in a wheelchair."

Imagining fiery Mrs. Haven in a wheelchair was difficult for Brittany. She'd been such a strong and vibrant presence around camp.

"What about your father? Is he well?"

"Very," answered Rory. "He coaches at Dartmouth, close to the hospital where my mother still receives care."

"And you took over here," she said.

"By default," he said softly, his forehead creasing.

She wondered what thoughts caused that wrinkle, hoping he'd tell her, but he didn't. "It looks like Summerhaven's doing well in its reincarnation as a conference center."

He lifted his gaze, meeting her eyes. "Yes. I mean, my parents had already opened up the campground for off-season conferences and events several years ago. When I came on board, I phased out the children's summer camping program and committed all of our incoming capital and resources to retrofitting the grounds and buildings into a rustic, yet luxurious, destination for conferences, meetings, team-building weekends, and hopefully, weddings."

"Hopefully," she said, smiling at him. "It looks wonderful. You're doing a great job."

"Thanks," he said, his gaze lingering on her face as Victor returned with their wine, placing a full glass in front of each of them.

"Your salads will be out in a few minutes."

"Thank you, Victor," said Rory, lifting his wineglass. "Speaking of weddings…congratulations on your engagement."

Brittany touched her glass to his before taking a sip,

unsurprised that it was crisp, cold, and excellent. "Thank you."

"And thank *you* for taking a look at Summerhaven as a possible venue."

"Want to know something strange? When I married Travis Mathison, it didn't even occur to me to get married at Summerhaven, even though we were campers here together. But as soon as Ben proposed, it was the first place that came to mind."

"What's Ben's full name?"

"Parker. Dr. Ben Parker. He's a pediatrician. In Boston."

"And he won't mind trekking to New Hampshire for his wedding?"

"He's left everything up to me," said Brittany, "so he better not."

"Okay, then," said Rory, watching her over the rim of his wineglass.

His smile was easy, but his eyes were intense, staring at her face like he was trying to reconcile his memories of teenage-her with adult-her. She wondered how she measured up against herself, although, to be honest, she was a bit surprised he'd recognized her at all. She doubted they'd exchanged more than a handful of words over the course of four summers.

Suddenly, he tilted his head to the side. "Can I ask you something?"

"Fire away," she said, taking another sip of wine.

"You're…twenty-seven? Like me?"

She nodded.

"I'm just curious, because—that seems young, you

know? To be married, divorced, and marrying again."

Some women may have been affronted by the baldness with which Rory Haven made this observation, but several of Brittany's friends had called her out on the exact same thing. She offered him the response she'd given them.

"Just because it didn't stick the first time doesn't mean it won't this time."

"Why didn't it?" he asked, toying with the stem of his glass, his eyes more interested than nosy. "Stick?"

Without giving it much thought, she opted for honesty. "I wanted kids. He didn't."

"And this time?"

"Ben's a pediatrician," she said, "and already a father. He loves kids."

Rory grinned at her, lifting his glass as though toasting her. "Good. I'm glad you'll have what you want this time."

She smiled back at him, although the nagging truth was that Brittany had never asked Ben point-blank if he wanted more children. Before he'd proposed, while they were still dating, it had seemed indelicate to ask him, and maybe she was even a little scared that mentioning kids would put too much pressure on them. And after he'd proposed, she'd simply chosen to believe that he wouldn't have asked her unless he wanted kids too.

She'd convinced herself—as she just had Rory—that a man who had children and loved children and treated children must want more. Besides, on the night they met, she was crying over wanting her own, so it was fair to assume that he knew her feelings about having children, and yet, he'd still pursued her.

He'd been a master at pursuing her, in fact.

There'd been romantic, candlelit dinners and impromptu knocks at her door after he'd finished a long shift. He'd pull her into his arms, undressing her in the foyer as he murmured that he couldn't be apart from her for another moment. He'd spoken several times at A Better Tomorrow, his warm words of encouragement and handsome smile endorsing long months of earned sobriety among the women Brittany wanted to help. Yes, indeed. Ben Parker was the most perfect boyfriend Brittany had ever had.

Once they'd gotten engaged, she meant to bring up having kids as they walked by a playground some lazy Sunday morning or after spending a day with his girls. But putting a ring on her finger hadn't accelerated their relationship, as she'd expected. In fact, sometimes it still felt like they were dating, not getting ready to plan a life together.

His work schedule dominated their lives in a way that had seemed dedicated at first and now seemed overbearing. *But if you marry a doctor*, she reasoned, *the cost will sometimes be putting yourself second. It's worth it, Brittany. It's worth it for a man like Ben Parker.*

Anyway, when he'd consented to the wedding date on Thursday night, the question of having children together had rushed to the forefront of her mind, but something—maybe her gratitude that they were finally pressing forward in *some* measure—had held her back from asking.

She recalled his words on the night they met, *I bet your babies will look like angels someday*, and exhaled the breath she was holding.

Of course he wants children. Of course he does.

She looked up at Rory Haven to find him watching her intently.

"Everything okay?" he asked.

She nodded. "How about you? Do you have kids? Want them?"

"Have them? No. Want them?" He grinned at her. "Yeah, of course. I'm Irish. It's one of our specialties."

"Breeding?" she blurted out.

"Ha! Breeding!" he chortled, his face splitting into a surprised grin. He raised his eyebrows at her, and she wished a hole in the floor would open and swallow her up. *Whole*. "Sure. I guess. I mean, I would've gone with something more delicate like 'big families,' but—"

"I could die." Brittany reached up to cup her flaming cheeks, shocked by her own rudeness. "I'm—I'm so sorry, Ror—I mean, Mr. Haven…Oh, God…"

Still laughing as Victor served their salads before slipping away, Rory caught her eyes over the rim of his wineglass. "Okay. First of all, no more *Mr. Haven*. It's Rory. Once two people talk about breeding over lunch, they must remain on a first-name basis for life."

Brittany's head drooped forward as she stared down at her lap with mortification.

"And second of all, there's nothing to be embarrassed about, Britt." He paused, taking a bite of salad. "It's all good. It was funny. Shake it off."

Britt.

Huh. Britt.

It had been a long, long time since anyone but Hallie had called her "Britt," and it made her pause because the girl once called Britt was so different from the woman who was Brittany.

Britt had been carefree and fun. She spent six weeks of

bliss at Summerhaven and loved every second. She had three best friends who had her back, who kept her secrets and believed in her. She was confident and witty—and sure, a little silly and sassy—but full of giggles and hugs. But most important of all, Britt wasn't lonely. She was loved. She *knew* that she was loved by three friends she adored like sisters.

Spearing a piece of grapefruit on her fork, Brittany rested it on the plate for a second as the old nickname continued to ping in her head, welcome—*so very, very welcome*—after so many years.

Looking up at Rory, who was eating his salad but still grinning in good-natured amusement, Brittany felt the scorching heat in her cheeks cool a little.

"You know what? I was called that when I summered here. Britt, not Brittany. When I was here, I was Britt."

"I know," he said, his deep-green eyes meeting hers, the rumble of his soft voice making something forgotten come alive inside of her. He nodded, his bright smile an unexpected balm to the uncertainness in her heart. "I remember."

After lunch, Rory took Brittany on a tour of the updated property, showing her the new gardens, gazebo, banquet hall, and chapel, chatting with her about her "dream wedding" and making mental notes about where she'd like to have the rehearsal dinner, ceremony, and reception.

She was cheerful and sure-footed beside him, exclaiming over things she remembered and offering compliments on his renovations. And though he doubted that Brittany Manion was much involved with the hotel chain her great-grandfather had started in the early 1900s, he still felt chuffed that a *Manion* was complimenting his work and vision.

When they got to Lady Margaret cottage in Oxford Row, Brittany squealed, running to the front door and holding out her hand for the key. "Can I go in?"

Charmed by her enthusiasm, he handed over the master key, letting her unlock the door and following her inside.

What had once been a small, semirustic cabin—with a crumbling fireplace, no electricity, two bunk beds, four small bureaus, four armoires, and a shared cold-water bathroom— had been beautifully upgraded.

The old fireplace had been rebuilt with fresh brick and mortar, and a soft, thick, sheepskin rug covered the shellacked pine floor. There were two queen-sized sleigh beds, also in pine, one on each side of the bathroom door, and covered in Frette sheets and expensive down duvets. And if she peeked into the bathroom, she'd find a modern waterfall shower and white marble vanity and countertops. The cottage was as luxurious as a double room in any five-star hotel, and Rory was proud as hell of the refurbishments.

But Brittany stood frozen in the doorway, as still as a statue.

"Britt?" he whispered.

She inhaled deeply, as though she'd been holding her breath. "It's all gone."

"Wh-What's gone?"

"Lady Margaret." She took another step into the cottage and gestured limply to the bed on the left. "The bunks. The…the little dressers. It's all gone."

"Oh," said Rory, swallowing his disappointment at her reaction. "Well, we couldn't very well ask corporate executives to sleep in bunk beds. We had to...you know, change things up."

But, dammit. It hadn't occurred to him that compromising her nostalgia might change her mind about having her wedding at Summerhaven. Shoot. He didn't want that to happen. He really needed her business.

"The beds are comfortable. *Really* comfortable, and guests are loving the waterfa—"

Still a little zoned out, she started speaking over him. "I think...I think when you love a place, you freeze it in your mind. You expect it to stay the same forever. And it would have, if I hadn't come back."

She was right. In her mind, this would have remained a musty-smelling, fireplace-crumbling cabin for four little girls with beat-up furniture from the 1940s and a cold-water spigot in the bathroom. Forever. Seeing it renovated had taken that away from her.

But Rory looked over her shoulder at the improvements. Despite her obvious disappointment, he couldn't bring himself to apologize for them. He'd put his heart into the changes at Summerhaven.

That said, however, he hadn't traded her nostalgia for her business. He could feel it slipping through his fingers.

"Well...I guess we should be getting back," he said, trying to keep the bitterness he felt out of his tone.

"It's very pretty," she said softly, letting her fingers touch down lightly on a duvet. "You did a nice job."

Then she turned and walked out of the cabin.

Rory followed her, his stomach in knots as he locked

the door and turned to face her. "…But you don't want to have your wedding here."

"I didn't say that."

He sighed, though it sounded unintentionally loud in his ears. More like a huff. "You didn't have to. It's not the place you remember."

Her brows furrowed. "I said it was pretty. I said you did a nice job."

"*Nice*. The kiss of death," said Rory under his breath.

"That's not—hey, wait. I'm not criticizing you, Rory. Give me a chance to grieve what I just lost, okay?"

Clenching his jaw together, he drew in a deep breath and exhaled again. They'd connected over lunch and she'd seemed genuinely impressed with the changes to the camp. Now? He was fairly certain his chance to break into top-shelf weddings via heiress Brittany Manion was gone, and his frustration roiled inside of him.

He'd paid his goddamned dues. He'd stayed here for years, when all he'd wanted was to strike out on his own. When would it be *his* turn? When would his life be his own?

"Well, that's that," he muttered.

"Rory?"

Certain his gaze would be stormy, he took another deep breath, blinking before he locked eyes with her and attempting a neutral smile. "Let me walk you back to your car."

"No more tour?"

"What's the point?"

She took a step toward him, her brown eyes clear and earnest. "I still want to book it for my wedding. That's the point."

"Wait. What? You do?"

She nodded, a small smile tilting her lips up. "Of course I still want to. Summerhaven's changed, but so have I. So have you." She paused, giving him a look. "Though you still brood like a champion."

"I *what* like a champion?"

"Brood." She screwed up her pretty face into an exaggerated grimace, lowering her voice to a growl. "Dark scowl. Narrowed eyes. Tight lips."

"I do *not* look like that," he protested.

"I wish I had a mirror," she said.

"So, you're still interested, huh?" He was still processing the fact that he hadn't lost her business after all.

"I'm still interested," she confirmed.

Just when Rory was about to suggest that they take a look at the Cambridge cabins before returning to the office so that he could take a deposit, his phone buzzed in his pocket. He withdrew it, glancing at the screen and cringing.

Tierney.

He looked up at Brittany. "Um…I'm sorry. I need to take this. It's an emergency."

Her eyes widened in concern. "Please. Go ahead."

Turning his back to his guest, he answered the call as he took a few steps away. "Tierney? What's up?"

"Ian, quit it!" she yelled half into the phone and half to their brother.

In the background, he could hear his brother throwing a tantrum: "*Go hifreann leat, Tierney!*" which translated to Ian telling their sister to go to hell, followed by "*Where are your goddamned, fucking keys?*" in English.

Glass was smashed against a wall, and from a loud

bang, he knew that some furniture followed.

"Jaysus, Ian!" yelled Tierney. "Stop it! You're not going anywhere!"

"Get out of there," said Rory, clenching his jaw in anger.

"Nah. He's just being an arsehole," said Tierney. "Woke up vomiting on my floor. Sweating all over. Shaking. He wants my keys to go buy himself a drink."

The DTs.

Deep tremors. Withdrawal.

If Ian hadn't had a drink since arriving at Tierney's last night a little after midnight, he'd been without a drink for about—he looked at his watch and noted it was almost three o'clock—*fifteen hours*. It only took six for withdrawal to start. Ian was fast approaching the stage of seizures and hallucinations.

"He's withdrawing."

"And how!" Again, her voice slid away. "If you break that, Ian McAllister Haven, I swear to Christ, I'll—" Something glass or ceramic fell to the floor with a crash and Tierney gritted out, *"Damnú!"*

"Get out of there, Tierney. Now."

"He won't hurt me, Rory. He wouldn't dare!"

"The fuck he won't."

"He *won't*. He's just wrecking my house on the excuse of looking for my keys."

"Fuck that. This is *totally* unacceptable. Put him on the phone."

"Rory, don't make it worse." She blew out a puff of breath. Her voice was smaller and softer when she spoke again. "But can you get here sooner?"

"Put him on the phone, Tier."

She was holding out the phone to their brother because their voices were muffled.

"Here. It's Rory."

"Fuck Rory. Give me your keys."

"Talk to Rory first."

"What?" shouted Ian into the phone.

Rory's voice was lethal. "You calm yourself the fuck down, brother. I'm coming up there in three minutes, and if you aren't the bloody picture of calm when I arrive, I'll put my fist through your gob and knock you out. Hear me?"

"Fuck you, Rory."

"No, Ian. Fuck you! You can't keep doing this."

"Then I'll go." The phone dropped onto the floor with a thud, and Rory heard Ian demand, "Give me my phone, Tierney, and I'll get an Uber to come pick me up."

"You can't have your phone right now. Why don't you go lie down?"

"Fuck you, Tierney! Why don't *you* go lie down?"

Rory ran a hand through his hair, hissing a string of curses before turning around to find Brittany Manion standing there, wide-eyed, mouth loosely open, obviously listening to his conversation. Fuck. He'd forgotten she was even there.

"Ah, *shite*!" he muttered. "Sorry."

"No!" she exclaimed. "Don't be sorry! Sounds serious."

"It is. My sister is—"

"Rory?" Tierney's voice was back on the phone.

Rory held Brittany's concerned brown eyes. "I'm here."

"He's gone back to throwing up. When can you get here?"

"I'll be there in twenty minutes."

"Bring Gatorade? And, um, saltines? And maybe some ice cream?"

"Dairy? He'll throw it up."

"He'll throw up anyway. At least that'll feel nice going down," said Tierney.

"Tierney!" sobbed Ian's voice from the bathroom.

"He's calling me. I've got to go."

"I'm coming now," said Rory, pocketing his phone.

There was no point in trying to smooth this over for Brittany Manion's benefit. Maybe he'd lose her business, or maybe he wouldn't, but right this minute, his siblings needed him, and he needed to be with them. "I need to go help my sister."

He stood there, frozen, his heart racing, dreading the next twelve to twenty-four hours with his brother.

Brittany reached for his hand, entwining her fingers through his and squeezing gently in a gesture of comfort.

She didn't say she was sorry. She didn't lift her chin in judgment. She didn't offer useless platitudes. But her eyes were soft and kind when she squeezed his hand again, then tugged on it, pulling him back up the path toward the office.

"Then let's go."

chapter five

Brittany didn't say a word as they walked briskly back to the office, hand in hand. She was distracted by the strong, warm grasp of Rory's fingers, all of her nerve endings unavoidably focused on their flush palms. What would she have given to be walking up the path like this with Rory Haven ten years ago?

Grow up, Brittany. He's in the middle of a crisis.

Whatever was going on with Ian Haven was bad.

She'd heard the word *withdrawing*, and she'd heard Rory threaten to "knock out" his brother. She didn't want to make assumptions, but based on the volunteer work she'd done with A Better Tomorrow, she was fairly certain that Ian Haven was a drug addict or an alcoholic going through the early stages of withdrawal.

Either way, it wasn't her business to ask.

But it *was* her mission to get Rory back to the office as quickly as possible.

As they approached the largest structure in the campground, Rory dropped her hand, running both hands through his hair. "Shit!"

"What?"

"I have a group coming. A—a corporate retreat. They'll start arriving in an hour."

As he muttered incoherent, curse-sounding, foreign words in an impressive string, Brittany rubbed her hands together. "From where?"

"Boston. The Crockett Group."

She knew of the Crockett Group. They were a private equity firm. Well respected. Old-school, but young.

"Leave it to me."

He looked up at her. "What are you talking about?"

"I can help. I can…greet guests, hand out keys, show them to their lodgings. I lived here for four summers and just got the grand tour. I know the campground like the back of my hand. Why not let me help?"

Rory gave her a long look, like her suggestion was utterly ridiculous, then walked right past her and up the stairs to the office, letting the screen door slam behind him. She hurried to follow him.

"Mrs. Toffle, I need to go to Tierney's, and Miss Manion is leaving," he was saying as she entered the office. "Can you call Doug and see if he can come in to help?"

"Doug's in Iceland," she answered. "Remember?"

"Who's Doug?" asked Brittany, stepping up to the counter with her hands on her hips.

"The assistant manager," said Mrs. Toffle. "He took a vacation before the season really started up in May."

"God damn it!" yelled Rory. "Mrs. Toffle, you'll need to welcome the guests and show them to their lodgings."

"But Mr. Haven," she said, "who will be here in the office to greet them and check them in?"

"What about one of the housekeeping staff? Or Victor! I'll go get Victor!"

"Victor the waiter?" asked Mrs. Toffle. "But the kick-off event is cocktails and dinner in the dining room from six until nine. Victor will be busy setting up."

"He can still take people to their cottages," insisted Rory. "There are six other waiters working the event tonight, *and* Chef Jamie and his staff."

"Does Victor know the camp that well?" asked Mrs. Toffle. "I've never seen him anywhere but the dining room."

"Give him a map!" said Rory.

"So he can fumble through walking them to their cottages?" asked Brittany.

"Then he can stay here in the office and greet them. Check them in!" thundered Rory.

The office seemed to shake with Rory's voice as Brittany looked up at Mrs. Toffle, who shook her head. "He doesn't know how to check them in on the computer. Only you, Doug, and I do."

"Mrs. Toffle," said Brittany in her best no-nonsense voice, rounding the counter to stand beside the receptionist's desk, "you will be in charge of greeting the guests and checking them in. I will show them to their cottages in small groups. Which rows are booked for tonight?"

"Cambridge and Oxford," said Mrs. Toffle.

"Excellent. My favorites. I assume I can use the golf carts out front for luggage?"

"Of course, Miss Manion," said the older lady, grinning at Brittany.

"Brittany," she said. "Or Britt. But I'll still call you Mrs. Toffle."

"Or Mrs. T," said Miranda, beaming at the younger woman.

Brittany turned to Rory and lifted her chin. "See? It's all

settled. Now stop bothering us and go help your sister."

His eyes were stricken. "I can't let you do this. I can't let a potenti—"

"A potential client help?" asked Brittany crisply. "Then consider this, Rory Haven: if you refuse my help, it will hurt my feelings and I *won't* book my wedding here. How does that sound?"

"Bad."

"Oh, dear. Very bad," added Mrs. Toffle. "If you don't book your wedding here, then Rory won't be able to—"

"Okay!" cried Rory, cutting off Mrs. Toffle.

Rory won't be able to…what?

"Mrs. Toffle," he said, "print a copy of the full roster and guest room assignments. Do we have another Summerhaven polo shirt? If we do, find it and give it to Britt." He turned to her. "The keys are up there on the board. The names are on the—"

"You do know my last name is *Manion*, right?" she said. "As in Manion Hotels? I can figure this out, Rory. It's in my blood. Now *please* go to Tierney."

"Damn Ian," muttered Rory. He shot a look to his receptionist. "You good with this, Mrs. Toffle?"

"Over the moon, dear."

Rory turned his attention from her to Brittany, scanning her face, his gaze resting for a split second on her lips before he met her eyes again. "I don't know how to thank you."

"I do. Stop wasting time and go help your sister," she said, trying desperately to ignore the billowing warmth in her stomach, which felt like the wings of a thousand butterflies flapping madly. "Just go."

He lurched forward and pressed his lips to her cheek.

"Thank you, Britt."

By the time she opened her eyes, he was gone.

Rory had driven from the camp in Center Sandwich to Tierney's place in Moultonborough a hundred times, but this afternoon he felt an added urgency to get there as soon as possible. He'd even hated having to stop at the convenience store for supplies.

Then again, he knew that Tierney was probably right: Ian wouldn't hurt her. They'd been through withdrawals twice before with him, and both times, even once when he was hallucinating, he hadn't hurt them. The biggest problem was, if he started seizing, Tierney wasn't strong enough to hold Ian down to ensure he wouldn't bang his head against the floor or a wall. He could seriously injure himself—causing a concussion, or worse.

Rory stepped on the gas.

He stopped at the main gates of Moonstone Manor, punching the code into the keypad and thrumming his fingers on the steering wheel as the gate slowly opened for him. Screeching through the gates as soon as there was enough space, he sped up the winding road through a small portion of the five-thousand-acre woods that led to the eighteen-room mountaintop estate, known locally as the "Palace in the Sky."

Turning off the main road, he pulled into a small gravel driveway and parked his truck beside Tierney's Grand Cherokee at the caretakers' cottage, where Tierney lived. Without knocking, he opened the Spanish-style wooden front door of the small stone dwelling and kicked it shut behind him.

The room before him was in total disarray: shards of broken glass were scattered on the floor. There was an overturned coffee table with two legs missing and a bookcase that had been yanked from the wall, littering the hardwood floor with books.

"Tierney?" he yelled.

"Up here."

Placing the paper sack of supplies on the floor at the foot of the staircase, he took the narrow steps two at a time to the second floor of her home, where there were two tiny bedrooms and a shared bathroom. Standing in the doorway, he covered his mouth at the scene he found, choking back a gag from the stench.

The floor was splashed with pinkish vomit in which Ian knelt, his head over the bowl of the toilet while Tierney sat on the side of the bathtub behind him, the knees of her jeans soaked with throw up and one weary hand rubbing her brother's back. As she looked up at Rory, her green eyes filled with tears.

"Ror. You came."

"Of course I came." He shrugged out of his jacket and threw it down the corridor, then took a deep breath of clean air before turning back to Tierney. "What do you need?"

Visibly shaken with a combination of grief and exhaustion after several hours of dealing with Ian, she blinked rapidly before clearing her throat and saying in a shaky voice, "I need to get a mop. Can you stay with him? Maybe clean him up and get him back in bed? I'll change the sheets, and then I'll mop up in here."

"How long has it been since he puked?"

Tierney stood up wearily. "About twenty minutes."

She sidestepped by him into the hallway and Rory swapped places with her, sitting down on the edge of the tub and reaching out to place his hand flat on Ian's back.

"Go get some air," said Rory to Tierney, who stood in the bathroom doorway. "I'll get him cleaned up and into bed. Come back in half an hour."

"I'm okay. I can get the bed ready."

"Tierney," said Rory, his green eyes boring into hers, "so can I. You're off duty. Go take a break."

Her face cracked for a second as she nodded, taking a deep, shaking breath before turning away. She left her brothers alone, her footsteps progressively softer as she headed downstairs.

Ian's hair was soaked with sweat and hardening bits of sour-smelling puke. He groaned softly into the toilet bowl, his voice low and rough. "Ror?"

"I'm here, Ian."

"You hate me?"

Rory clenched his jaw, surprised by the tears that suddenly burned his eyes. He shook his head, his hand reaching for the back of Ian's neck, his warm, dry palm flush against his brother's clammy skin.

"I love you, Ian. We both do." He rubbed his brother's neck. "That's why this sucks."

"Sorry, bro."

"I know," said Rory, swallowing back a million other things he wanted to say about how Tierney deserved an apology and how Ian was going to fix every fucking thing he broke downstairs and how much he wanted Ian to kick this addiction and how much he wanted his funny, mischievous brother back. "I know, Ian."

They sat together in silence for a few minutes before Rory spoke again. "How about a shower?"

"I can't move, bro. Everything hurts."

"I'll help you."

Under his hand, Rory felt his brother's great shoulders shudder, and a loud sob echoed into the toilet. "I'm such a *fucking asshole.*"

Rory blinked back his own tears. "Yeah. But we already knew that. Old news."

Ian's sob was punctuated by a chuckle. "You're an asshole too."

"Takes one to know one." Putting his hands under Ian's shoulders, Rory pulled him up to a seated position.

Ian looked over his shoulder and Rory was careful to keep his expression neutral, though it was difficult. His brother's long dark hair was slick with sweat, dirty and speckled with puke. And his eyes—his bright-green emerald eyes—were soupy, bloodshot, and tired. They were the eyes of a man twice Ian's age and just as world weary.

"That bad, huh?" asked Ian.

Rory gulped. "I've seen worse."

"You're a shit liar."

Rory stood up and turned on the shower, reaching out his hand to be sure it was warm, but not too hot. Then he turned back to Ian. "I'll help you up, okay?"

Ian grunted, bracing his hands on the toilet seat as Rory put his hands under Ian's shoulders and pulled him up. Because Ian was bigger than Rory by a couple of inches and a good thirty pounds, it was no easy feat, and his brother swayed on his feet as soon as he was standing. Rory braced him again the wall beside the shower, reaching for the button and zipper of his brother's jeans. He hooked his thumbs into Ian's boxers and pushed both filthy, stinking items to the floor, making a mental note to tell Tierney to burn them. Then he unbuttoned Ian's flannel shirt, avoiding his brother's eyes. He didn't want Ian to see the profound grief in them, the intense sadness.

When his brother was naked, Rory gestured with his chin to the shower. "Ready?"

Ian searched Rory's face. "I hate myself."

Rory nodded. "I know."

"I want to stop," said Ian, tears sliding down his dirty face into his unkempt beard. "I just don't know if I can."

"Fuck that," said Rory, reaching forward to wipe Ian's tears away. "You can do anything you set your mind to. Now get in the shower."

He pulled back the curtain and held Ian's elbow as he stepped over the lip of the tub into the stream of warm water.

"You good? You steady?" asked Rory.

"Yeah. I'm going to stay in here for a little bit."

Rory opened the cabinet under Tierney's sink and found a spray bottle of bathroom cleaner and a clean face cloth. He sprayed down the toilet and wiped up the worst of the puke, occasionally peeking in the shower to be sure Ian hadn't fallen asleep.

When the toilet was clean-ish, he sat down on the lid, glancing at his watch.

Four thirty.

The guests were arriving now, and he briefly wondered

how Mrs. Toffle and Brittany were doing.

Brittany.

Britt.

She was some sort of a miracle today with her willingness—no, *instance* on helping. Had she always been that nice? That kind? He wished he knew. He wished like hell he'd defied his parents ten years ago and gotten to know her a little bit when they were teenagers.

"Rory?"

"Yeah, man. I'm here."

"Just making sure."

"Ian, you want to eat something? I got ice cream."

"No, thanks."

Rory shoved the curtain aside to check on his brother, who stood upright in the shower with his forehead against the tile wall under the spray. His body sported bruises in all stages—red and blue, purple and greenish-yellow—which meant he'd probably taken a few beatings recently. Rory winced, then pulled the curtain shut again.

"Where you been living, Ian?"

"Here and there."

Rory had heard this before. It was code for "homeless."

"On the street?"

Ian made a noncommittal grunting noise.

"In Boston?"

After a few seconds passed, Ian asked, "Does it really matter?"

"Nope."

"Tierney's shampoo smells like a girl."

"So you'll smell like a girl," said Rory. "It's an improvement on smelling like shit. Wash your hair."

The smell of Tierney's shampoo mixed with the scents of Lysol and puke, and Rory looked at the floor and walls. Ian's aim hadn't been very good this time. Rory sighed. He'd help Tierney give the bathroom a thorough scrubbing once Ian was safely in bed.

"What's your plan, Ian?"

"I don't know."

At least Ian hadn't told him to fuck off, which was generally what happened at this point in the conversation. "Well, you're at—what?—sixteen or seventeen hours now? How about we try to make that twenty-four?"

Ian was quiet for a few minutes before speaking, his voice low and soft when he asked, "How about we try to make it forever?"

Rory had been resting his cheek on his palm, but now he sat up straight on the toilet lid, staring at Tierney's flowered shower curtain in surprise. He couldn't remember the last time Ian was open to recovery, and his heart beat faster at the idea of helping Ian get clean.

"What?"

"I'm sick of this. I—I don't want to *be* this. I look like shit. I feel like shit. I want to get well."

Rory leaned forward. "Do you...do you mean it, Ian?"

"Yeah, but I can't do it alone."

"You don't have to."

Ian turned off the water, but the curtain still separated the brothers.

"I might not make it," whispered Ian.

"We'll help you," said Rory, standing up, trying desperately to temper his excitement at Ian's words. "Tierney and I—we're ready to help you. I swear."

"I might disappoint you."

"I don't care. We won't know unless you try."

Rory grabbed a towel from the small cabinet behind the bathroom door and pulled back the curtain. Ian's green eyes, bright with tears in his ruddy, bearded face, looked into Rory's as he took the towel and wrapped it around his waist.

"Do you want to try, Ian?"

"Yeah," he said softly. "I want to try."

Tears flooded Rory's eyes again as he helped Ian out of the shower and walked him into Tierney's guest bedroom.

Even though he'd told her not to, she'd obviously scrubbed the floor and changed the sheets while Ian was in the shower. The room was neat as a pin and smelled of recently sprayed air freshener, which mostly covered up the latent odor of vomit.

Rory opened the bottom drawer of the dresser and took out a pair of men's sweats and a T-shirt that Tierney left there for her brothers. He helped Ian get dressed, then pulled back the crisp, clean sheets and tucked his brother into the center of the bed, lying down beside him.

"Room for me?"

The brothers looked over to see Tierney, in clean clothes, standing in the doorway.

"I'm fucking sorry, Tier," said Ian, his voice breaking as tears streamed from the corners of his eyes into his wet, clean hair. "*Tá brón orm.*"

Tierney lay down on Ian's other side, stared at the ceiling for a second, then took his hand in hers and whispered, "*Tá grá agam ort,* Ian."

Ian sniffled, reaching for Rory's hand on his other side. "I love you too. Both of you."

After a few quiet moments, Rory said, "Ian wants to get clean."

"Huh," muttered Tierney.

"I mean it," said Ian. "I really mean it this time, Tier."

Tierney took a deep breath, held it, then let it go. "You've meant it before."

"Not like this," said Ian. "I want to get clean. I'm willing to do the work. I swear."

When Tierney spoke again, her voice was shaky and emotional. "Okay."

"You'll help me?" he asked.

"A hundred times," said Rory.

"A thousand times," amended Tierney, turning to her side on the comforter and resting her forehead on Ian's shoulder.

Branch-shaped shadows danced on the ceiling in the late-afternoon setting sun.

"Better together," said Rory. Then he added, as their mother used to when she wanted to remind them of their special triplet bond, "*Trí ciarde.*"

You're not just brothers and sister. You're not just family. That's too easy because you were born with each other. You need to work at it. You need to be friends too. Three friends. Trí ciarde.

"*Trí ciarde,*" said Tierney, a tentative smile in her voice.

"*Trí ciarde,*" whispered Ian, taking a deep, clean breath before falling fast asleep.

chapter six

Rory napped with his siblings for an hour or so before getting up to help Tierney clean the bathroom and put her cottage back together after Hurricane Ian had ripped through. The damage was less than it had initially appeared: an antique vase was shattered beyond repair, but the ceramic pots Ian had broken might have a chance with Krazy Glue. He'd also busted the bookcase and coffee table, but it looked like those could be fixed.

By nine o'clock, Ian had held down some Gatorade and saltines, and though he still sweated and shook in bed, it had been more than twenty hours since his last drink. He'd still feel like shit for two or three more days, but it appeared that he'd sidestepped seizures this time. The worst was over.

But now the *real* work began—helping him stay clean.

"Ian, how about you stay with Tierney for a while? Help her get Moonstone ready for the summer crowds?"

"Yeah, I could do that."

"There's lots to be done," said Tierney. "And I could pay you a little too."

"There's an 8:00 pm meeting at the Moultonborough Methodist Church tomorrow," said Rory, who'd looked up the local AA schedule. "I'll come get you. We'll go together, okay?"

Ian nodded his head against the pillow, his eyes starting to close again. "Yeah. Good. Thanks, Ror."

Rory leaned down and pressed his lips to his brother's sweaty forehead before leaving, sending up a quick prayer of thanks to God that Ian was still alive and motivated to get clean. *Please let it stick this time.*

He hugged Tierney hard on his way out.

"You're a rock star," he said.

"Ah, go on." She cocked her head to the side. "You think he can do it?"

"I can't remember the last time he really wanted to."

"Me neither."

"We'll do everything we can, huh?"

She nodded. "I'm on board."

"Me too." Rory sighed. "I've got to get back to camp."

"Did you get Doug to come in to help?"

"He's in Iceland. I got…someone else."

"On such short notice?" Tierney's brows furrowed. "Who?"

"No one you know," said Rory, opening her front door and stepping onto the stoop. He turned to look back at her. "Call me if you need me?"

"He'll be all right now," she said. "See you Sunday night?"

He nodded.

"Come at seven," said Tierney. "We'll have dinner first."

"Shepherd's Pie?"

She grinned, the first smile she'd cracked all day. "If you're lucky."

"We're Irish," said Rory, winking at her. "Aren't we

supposed to have luck covered?"

Parking behind the office at Summerhaven fifteen minutes later, he checked his watch, grimacing to find it was after nine thirty. *Britt's long gone by now,* he thought, with a wave of inexplicable melancholy. He would have liked to thank her. Hell, he would have just liked to see her lovely, expressive face one more time.

…Which means it's best that she's gone, he thought ruefully. *No need to get infatuated over Brittany Manion all over again.*

Mrs. Toffle looked up as he entered the dimly lit office.

"You're still here, Mrs. T?" he asked. "You should have gone home by now! It's late."

"You caught me on the way out." She turned off her desk light and stepped around the counter. "How's Ian?"

"Better. Asleep."

"How bad was it?"

"Really bad," he admitted, "although he said he wants to get clean."

Mrs. Toffle's sympathetic eyes brightened. "Well, that's progress."

"I guess." Rory shrugged. "I don't want to get my hopes up."

"When have you ever?" she asked, sliding her purse to her elbow.

"What does that mean?"

"It means give yourself a break, Rory Haven. Life isn't *guaranteed* to break your heart. If you lean in and trust it a little, it just might surprise you."

"What do you mean by tha—"

"Sometimes good things just happen. When they do, why don't you give them a chance?" He opened the door for her as she approached it, but she stopped beside him, looking up into his eyes. "Speaking of good things…I almost forgot to mention: Miss Manion is upstairs. I made up Tierney's room for her." She cocked her head to the side, mumbling to herself as she stepped onto the porch. "She's quite something, isn't she?"

Rory's whole body reacted to this news, lurching forward as he put his hand on Mrs. Toffle's shoulder. "Wait. What?"

"She's staying overnight. I knew you would insist. She was practically asleep on her feet by the time she finished work, and I told her she couldn't drive back to Boston in the dark," explained Mrs. Toffle, turning back around to face him. "She worked nonstop from three until nine—greeting guests, showing them to their cottages, seeing to their needs. She set up the AV equipment and microphone in the dining hall. She even made a short speech welcoming the attendees to Summerhaven. She was…well, she was remarkable."

"And she's upstairs," he reconfirmed, his eyes darting to the ceiling before searching Mrs. Toffle's eyes carefully.

"Yes," she said, a sly smile playing on her lips. She turned back around and stepped off the porch, into the night. "Good night, Mr. Haven."

"Good night, Mrs. Toffle," he murmured, locking the door behind her.

She's here. Britt's still here.

Resisting the urge to take the stairs three at a time, he turned off the office light and made his way upstairs quickly, but quietly, just in case she was already asleep. He unlocked the door and toed off his boots on the welcome mat, hanging his jacket on a peg across from the door. Tiptoeing into the living room, the first thing he saw was her waves of blonde hair hanging over the back of the couch.

Rounding the coffee table, he found her curled up on the couch in front of a crackling fire, wearing Tierney's old pajamas. With her eyes closed, her lips lightly opened, and her cheek resting on the back of his parents' old flowered couch, Brittany Manion took his breath away.

Who was this woman who'd spent the last six hours of her life helping him? She didn't really know him and certainly didn't owe him anything, and yet she'd saved him. She'd swooped in without hesitation and saved the day with humor and kindness and grace.

Reaching his hand to his chest, he flattened his palm over his heart, surprised by the sudden and intense ache there. He knew instinctively that it was a dangerous sensation, this wave of longing, of awe and gratitude, mixed with a decade-old attraction that was renewing by the second. If he could have stopped his feelings, he would have, but they overcame him mercilessly in waves of undiluted adoration. They took root deep inside of him—uselessly, because she was engaged to someone else—so many tiny tendrils sprouting from foolish seeds.

"Hey, you," she breathed, her eyes fluttering open and her sweet lips tilting up into a dreamy smile. "You're back. How's Ian?"

Rory blinked at her. *Speak. Say something.*

"B-Better."

"Better's good," she said. Then she yawned, chuckling as she covered her mouth with the back of her hand. "Sorry. Tired."

"Don't be sorry," he said, sitting on the coffee table

across from her, his knees almost touching her bare feet, which peeked over the edge of the couch. "Mrs. Toffle said you were amazing tonight."

"I had fun."

"Schlepping all over camp?"

"Mmm-hmm." She nodded, her voice low and sleepy, her heavy eyes at half-mast. "Schlepping all over camp."

"Ready for bed?" he asked.

She blinked at him and suddenly her eyes flashed open—wide, dark-brown orbs locking on his. "For b-bed?"

He cocked his head to the side. "Mrs. Toffle made up my sister's bed for you."

"Oh. Right. Yes," she said, averting her eyes as she leaned forward and stood up, crossing her arms over her chest. He caught the two spots of pink on her cheeks when she looked down at him. "Thank you."

Wait. Had she thought he was offering to share *his* bed? A brief image of naked Brittany Manion, with her blonde hair spread over his pillows like a halo, made his breath catch. He shifted uncomfortably where he still sat on the coffee table, facing a now-empty couch.

Quit it, you idjit. She's engaged.

She was halfway down the hallway when he called out to her.

"Britt!"

She looked at him over her shoulder. "Yes?"

"I forgot to say thank you. For everything."

"My pleasure," she said, a smile blooming on her face before she turned back around, opening the door to Tierney's old room. "Night, Rory."

She stepped inside, and the door latched shut behind

her.

"*Oíche mhaith…mo mhuirnín,*" he murmured, rooted where he stood, staring down the dark hallway where the star of his hottest teenage dreams was spending the night.

Good night…my sweetheart.

Brittany awoke to the pitter-patter of rain and the smell of brewing coffee, one melding seamlessly with the other and heightening a dreamy feeling of bliss. Snug and warm under soft, sweet-smelling sheets and a puffy down duvet, she burrowed into her pillow, opening her eyes slowly to the soft gray light of daybreak filtering in through Tierney Haven's bedroom window.

Reaching for her iPhone, she checked the time—6:53 am—then replaced her phone on the nightstand and wiggled back under the covers. Except her eyes wouldn't stay closed, despite the rhythmic rain and warm, cozy bed. The coffee smelled too good, and there was only one person who could be brewing it: Rory Haven.

"Mmmm," she hummed softly, thinking of the way he had been looking at her when she opened her eyes last night.

Rory had grown into the kind of man that every woman wanted—tall and strapping, with dark hair and bright-green eyes; he was mature and responsible and unafraid to love the people who mattered to him. The way he left the campground yesterday, prioritizing his family over work, had left an indelible impression on Brittany. Old-fashioned words like *loyalty*, *honor*, and *character* circled in her head and made her feel lonely. One day, some lucky girl was going to land Rory Haven, and all that goodness would belong to her.

While Brittany would belong to Ben.

Wonderful Ben, she amended quickly.

Suddenly eager to connect with her fiancé, Brittany sat up and grabbed her phone again, swiping the screen to check for messages.

E-mails? Yes. A little number 5 in a red bubble raised her hopes. She pressed the app with anticipation, releasing a sigh of disappointment when she discovered they were all junk.

Calls? None.

Texts? None.

She sighed, cold discontent creeping into her warm, comfy morning.

Be reasonable, she told herself. *You and Ben almost never e-mail, call, or text while he's working a double. He's too busy, and you know it.*

And yet...

She still felt bothered. She'd slept somewhere else last night and he had no idea. Shouldn't he have known where she was? Shouldn't they have connected? Why shouldn't he call her just to say hello? She was his fiancée, after all. A text to say "Miss you. Love you. Good night" would literally take less than ten seconds to type, but it would let her know that she was on his mind, that he was thinking of her.

Unless he wasn't.

Now, if he was thinking about his young patients, immersed in thoughts of their care and treatment? She could accept that. Cheerfully, even. But even Brittany wasn't that naïve. Everyone had ten unspoken-for seconds in their day. Ben just didn't choose to spend them on her.

A soft rap at the door jolted her from her unsettling thoughts.

"Britt?" whispered a husky, morning-voiced Rory. "You up? If yes, there's coffee and I'm making biscuits. If no, sleep in."

She placed her phone back on the nightstand, screen down, and hopped out of bed, opening the door.

Rory stood in the hallway, his thick hair sleep-tousled, a rogue, dark-brown lock resting on his forehead. He wore a long-sleeved, navy-blue T-shirt pushed up to his elbows, with blue-and-gray plaid flannel pants. Her eyes, drawn to a vein that wound around his muscled forearm, stared for a moment before she jerked her head up, blinking up at him.

"Good morning."

He smiled at her. "Good morning." He ran a hand through his hair, then gestured to the kitchen with a flick of his neck. "Coffee?"

"Mm-hm," she hummed, but stepping from Tierney's carpeted room to the hardwood hallway floor made her gasp. "Cold!"

"Wait," said Rory, placing his hands on her hips and pushing her back a step.

He slid his hands away and sidestepped past her into Tierney's room, opening his sister's closet and bending down. When he stood up, he was holding a pair of leather slippers lined with fluffy sheepskin. "Put these on."

Her body had reacted when he'd reached for her, hyperaware of where he touched her—her breath stolen by the sweet and simple intimacy of it. It left her, inexplicably, longing for more.

I'm attracted to Rory...but I shouldn't be. The thought flitted through her head, but she silenced it, ignored it, reaching for the slippers that dangled from his fingers.

"Thanks," she said.

"Floors are cold year-round," he said. "It's nice in August."

The timer on the oven started beeping and Rory grinned. "Biscuits. Don't expect anything too fancy. They're the kind that come in the Pillsbury tube, but I've got comp'ny butter and honey too."

Following him into the kitchen, with Tierney's slippers scuffling softly with her steps, Brittany asked, "What's 'company' butter?"

"Oh," he said, putting on mitts before opening the oven door, "it's butter that's been left out on the counter all night so it softens. Spreads really easily."

"Slutty butter," she murmured, then clapped a hand over her mouth. "I don't know where that came from!"

"Ha!" He chuckled in surprise, shaking his head in bemusement. "*Slutty butter.* You're…different from what I thought."

Different. Right. I make totally inappropriate comments about breeding and promiscuous food items. I'm different, all right.

"It doesn't go bad? The butter?" asked Brittany, turning her back to him as she took the empty mug beside the coffeepot and poured herself a cup.

"Bad?" Rory placed a cookie sheet of six browned biscuits on the counter. "Nope."

When she turned to look at him, a mischievous smile played on his face, making his eyes sparkle. Likely, he was about to make a joke about "bad" butter, but she was grateful he didn't. She was embarrassed enough as it was.

He gestured to the table and they sat down across from each other, Rory sliding a white ceramic plate to her that held one perfect buttermilk biscuit. Opening the flaky layers, she inhaled deeply as the butter-flavored steam rose to her nose. Spreading some butter on the hot bread, she watched it melt and pool immediately, her mouth watering.

"Looks good, right?" he asked, pushing the honey to her. "Have some of this too. It's local."

She took the honey wand from the little pot and drizzled some over the biscuit, watching it seep into the buttery layers. "I never eat carbs, but this looks amazing."

As she bit into it, a stream of hot, buttery honey escaped down her chin and she reached for a paper napkin, dabbing at her face.

"Taking a bath in it, huh?" said Rory, grinning at her.

"It's messy."

"But tasty," he said, leaning over his plate to take another bite. "Why don't you eat carbs?"

Ben had once made a comment to her about how petite women needed to be careful about what they ate, because it didn't take long for them to balloon once they started eating whatever looked good. She'd weighed in the next morning to find that she'd gained a few pounds over the months they'd been dating. After that, she went on a strict no-carbs diet, and Ben hadn't mentioned her weight again.

"Don't you find slim women more attractive?"

"Is that what your fiancé wants? A *slim* woman?" he asked, his tone cool.

The answer was yes, but she sidestepped his question out of loyalty to Ben. "I think that's what most men want."

"Then I guess I'm not most men," said Rory, his eyes

darkening as he stared at her over biscuits, slutty butter, and honey, "because I like a woman to *look* like a woman…and that means curves."

Brittany's breath caught as she got lost in his stormy forest-green eyes. "Really?"

Rory nodded slowly, his eyes locked with hers. "Yeah. Really."

Ruffled by this intense attention, Brittany picked up her coffee mug, concentrating on the warm ceramic in her hands as she took a sip. When she looked up, Rory was drizzling more honey on his biscuit.

"So," she asked, "what's on the docket for today?"

Rory glanced up between bites. "Breakfast at nine in the north dining room, followed by a presentation. If the rain stops after lunch, Sven and Klaus are leading them in a ropes course. Trust exercises."

"Sven and Klaus?"

"These German brothers who live down in Meredith. They own an adventure business. I hire them for groups."

"I didn't know Summerhaven had a ropes course."

Rory nodded. "I added it. Corporate types love it."

"Ah-ha. And then?"

"Afternoon break-out sessions in the south dining room and barn, free time for all attendees, and then the farewell dinner in the north dining room at six. They leave after breakfast on Sunday morning."

"Whew," said Brittany, taking another sip of her coffee. "Busy agenda."

Rory nodded, glancing at his watch, then at the leftover biscuits. "You know what? It's only seven fifteen. I think I'll run over to Tierney's real quick. Bring them breakfast."

"Oh," said Brittany, assuming this was her cue to pack up and hit the road. "Well, thanks for having me overnight."

Rory was taking their dishes to the sink, but he spun around, his eyebrows furrowed. "You don't *have* to go yet, do you?"

"I thought—"

"No," said Rory. "You're welcome here. You can stay as long as you like…I mean, unless you *need* to get back."

But A Better Tomorrow was in good hands, and her only real "job" from now until Memorial Day weekend was to plan her wedding. Not to mention, with Ben working, she didn't have anyone to go home to.

"You wouldn't mind if I stayed another night?"

"Not at all," said Rory, his face softening, his eyes holding hers. "My rushing off to help Tierney cut short our meeting yesterday. If you don't have to go yet, I'm happy to introduce you to two local florists. And, let's see…Pastor Greene at the Congregational Church has officiated in the chapel here in the past. We could swing by his church to check his schedule too. And there's a photographer in Holderness who's quite good. We could go see her too."

"Yes! I'd like that," said Brittany, offering him a smile. She tilted her head to the side. "But first, could I…"

"Could you…?"

"Could I go with you? To see Tierney and Ian?"

She didn't know what had prompted her to make such a request of him; she remembered Ian as a mischievous troublemaker and Tierney as an introvert. Maybe it was just curiosity, or maybe she wanted the chance to see Rory with his siblings. She'd had so little experience with family, and theirs had always fascinated her.

Rory sighed. "Ian's not going to look good."

"One of the foundations I started in Boston is called A Better Tomorrow. We work with recovering addicts, helping them get their lives back on track once they've chosen sobriety," she said gently. "I don't have any expectations. I just...I don't know. Maybe a visit would cheer him up? I'd just like to help."

Her words rang in her ears, absurd and embarrassing to her as she reviewed them. She didn't know Ian Haven. She wasn't a doctor. She was an heiress who'd thrown some money at a few good causes. That didn't mean Rory Haven would or should feel comfortable bringing her to his sister's house to visit his brother.

Her cheeks and earlobes burned, no doubt scarlet. Why would Ian Haven want a visit from some girl he probably didn't even remember? God, how incredibly presumptuous of her to even ask.

"I'm out of line," she said in a rush. "I shouldn't have suggested it."

But when she looked up at Rory, he was staring at her with a soft expression, his eyes almost tender.

"Not at all," he said softly, taking a step toward her. "I'm glad you did. I'd love for you to come."

CHAPTER SEVEN

If anything can lift Ian's mood and encourage his sobriety, thought Rory as his truck bumped over the dirt path form the office to Summerhaven's exit, *it's a visit from beautiful Brittany Manion.*

At least, that was Rory's hope.

Unlike Rory, who'd followed their mother's instructions about "no fraternizin'" to the letter, Ian had secretly dated a couple of Summerhaven campers during his teen years, though Rory was fairly certain that Brittany wasn't on the list. Fairly.

Hmm. He glanced over at her, wearing the same chic clothes she wore yesterday, and grimaced. The idea of Ian and Brittany together—ten years ago or at any other time—made Rory want to clench his fists and slam them in Ian's face.

"Hey," he said, eyes on the road, "you, uh, you never dated my brother, did you?"

"*Irresistible* Ian?" she asked, invoking the nickname Rory had often heard whispered. "No, sir," she said, shaking her head. "I might have been a relatively naïve teenager, but I knew trouble when I saw it."

"And Ian was trouble?"

She turned to him, giving him a deadpan look. "Do bears poop in the woods?"

Rory chortled merrily, surprised to hear the word *poop* drop from Brittany's lips. "Yes. Yes, they do."

"Besides," she said, grinning at him for a moment before looking out the window, "he wasn't my type."

Who is?

The question sat right on the tip of Rory's tongue, but he swallowed it. He already knew the answer: Boston doctors with successful careers who liked their women skinny.

"Tell me about your fiancé," he said, already disliking the guy more than he had a right to.

"Umm…well, he's a doctor."

"Right. You told me that."

"And he has two daughters."

"Yep. That too." He adjusted his grip on the steering wheel as he turned onto the main road. "How'd you meet? What's he like?"

"Oh," she said, clearing her throat. "We met at a bar on New Year's Eve. He, um, he works a lot. He's an emergency room pediatrician."

Rory was silent. Maybe she was just warming up to the topic, but she wasn't really telling him much. If anything, she was giving him a brief résumé of Dr. Not-Good-Enough, not a sketch of their relationship, which was what he wanted.

"What do you two do for fun?"

"We, um…well, when he's not working, we have dinner together. And, you know, watch TV or read before bed."

"Does he play sports?"

"Yes! He's on a hospital softball league."

"And you?"

"I love skiing, but Ben doesn't ski, so…"

86

So you don't anymore. Well, that sucks. Couldn't he have made the effort to learn?

"I love skiing too."

"You practically have to, living in New Hampshire," she said, grinning at him for a moment. She looked out the window and sighed. "I guess we don't *do* a whole lot together, but he's a good man. He saves children for a living, and he doesn't mind, you know, about me. About who I am."

"Doesn't mind about what? What *are* you?"

"I'm…" She gestured to herself loosely with her hands, finally placing one palm flat on her chest. "…you know…"

Rory idled at a stoplight, turning to look at Brittany. "A gorgeous, smart, kindhearted woman?"

She gasped softly, eyes wide, her parted lips tilting up in a growing smile. "You're very nice."

"I'm just being honest."

She dropped Rory's eyes, staring down at her lap for a moment before looking up. "Ben doesn't mind that I'm a Manion."

Rory wasn't positive he hadn't heard her correctly. "Excuse me?"

"That I'm a Manion. He doesn't mind."

"*Mind?* Why would he mind in the first place?"

"Are you kidding?" she asked, her voice so low and serious it made a knot form in his stomach.

"No. I'm not kidding." *Why the fuck would Dr. Douche give a shit what her last name is? What does it matter?*

"Do you have any idea how many times Paris Hilton has broken up with someone because they were just using her to further their own interests? She *just* got engaged. At thirty-six. I mean, that's not young, Rory! Her sister, Nicky, married a financier a few years ago. Someone as wealthy as she is—no doubt in part so that she wouldn't have to worry about his motives. Some men are intimidated by it—the name, the money, the hotels, the fame—and others just want to use you," she said, taking a deep, ragged breath and letting it go slowly.

He'd hit a soft spot. He owed her an apology.

"Britt, I'm sorry. I didn't realize—"

"Ben's financially comfortable," she continued. "He makes a good living as a doctor *and* he has a bit of inherited money. I don't have to worry about him."

But is he right for you? Why was it that Rory couldn't shake the feeling that Ben was all wrong for her?

"I get it…" said Rory.

"So, you understand why I—"

"…but I also think you could be letting fear make your decisions. You're a Manion. Okay. Fine. But you're a lot more than a last name, Britt. You saved my ass yesterday. And this morning, you offered to come and cheer up my brother. You're kind and you're helpful, and I think…I mean, I don't know you *that* well, and you could be a nightmare in disguise, but…"

Her brown eyes seized on his, hanging on his words. "But what?"

"From what I can tell, you seem pretty awesome. And frankly, I care more about who you are than who you're related to."

The light changed to green, and he pressed on the gas as she shifted slowly in her seat to face him. He felt her eyes on him, steady and searching. In his peripheral vision, he could see the swell of her breasts rise and fall, as though testing the air between them, like it could tell her if he was being truthful. When he didn't look back at her, she rested her back against the seat once again, facing front.

"A nightmare in disguise, huh?" Her voice was warm and soft, tinged with humor. "What does *that* look like?"

Nothing like you. You're all daydream, mo mhuirnín.

Pulling up the gate at Moonstone Manor, he punched in his code, recalling Brittany's use of Ian's old nickname, "Irresistible Ian." He doubted that his brother would be very irresistible today. As the old gates opened, he turned to her, eyebrows raised in warning.

"I think you're about to find out."

After parking, Rory hopped out of the truck, then circled it to open Brittany's door, offering her his hand and grateful when she took it. It was small and soft in his, and when she stepped out of the truck and dropped it, the contact ended all too soon.

"Remember," he said as they approached the cottage, suddenly worried about the greeting she was about to receive, "he's only been—"

"Damn, Rory!" boomed Ian's voice. "Who's this fine piece of woman?"

Snapping his neck toward Tierney's house, Rory found Ian, in sweat pants and a T-shirt with a patchwork quilt around his shoulders, holding the door open. Ian didn't look great—his skin was sort of a grayish color, and his eyes were weary and bloodshot—but he grinned wolfishly at Brittany, then winked at Rory.

"Ian," said Rory. "Behave yourself, eh?"

Ian snorted at his brother, refocusing his attention on

Brittany. "I am the much more handsome and much more fun of the famous Haven brothers. *Ian* Haven. And you are?"

"Brittany Mathison—er, Manion."

"All *riiiight*." Ian's eyes took a leisurely sweep of her body. "Brittany Manion."

"In the flesh," she answered. She stood on the stoop outside the cottage with her back to Rory, facing Ian. Over her shoulder, Rory gave his brother a look, telling him to back—*the fuck*—off, and stepped a little closer to Britt.

"And what beautiful flesh it is," crooned Ian, who didn't give a shit that Rory was staring daggers at him. He stepped aside so they could enter Tierney's living room. "Come in, Brittany Manion. Come in."

"Is that Rory?" called Tierney from upstairs.

"Yeah," said Ian over his shoulder, adding, "and Brittany Manion."

"What? Brittany who?"

"Manion," shouted Ian, looking back and forth between Rory and Brittany with a devilish look in his eyes.

"Brittany Manion from camp?"

"You went to Summerhaven!" exclaimed Ian. "I *knew* I recognized your name! You know, beyond the hotels."

Footsteps landed on the stairs, and Tierney suddenly appeared. She stared at Brittany for a moment, then slid her eyes to Rory. One thing was for certain: she wasn't happy.

"What's this, now?"

"Tierney, meet Brittany."

Tierney had a roll of paper towels in her hand, which she set down on the bottom step as she approached her brothers. She wiped her hands self-consciously on her jeans before offering one to Brittany.

"I'm Tierney."

"I remember you," said Brittany gently, shaking Tierney's hand. "It's nice to see you again."

"Where's *my* handshake?" whined Ian.

Brittany crossed her arms over her chest and turned to Ian. "I'm not sure if it's nice to see *you.*"

"Oh, hell!" Ian grinned. "Why's that?"

"You don't really remember me, do you?" asked Brittany.

"Well, I recognize your name, of course, and you obviously went to Summerhaven at some point because Tierney remembers you, but no...I guess I can't *exactly* place you." He stepped closer to her, his grin suggestive as his eyes scanned her face. "Should I? Am I forgetting something memorable?"

"I was best friends with *Hallie*," said Brittany.

To Rory's surprise, and satisfaction, Ian's smile instantly dimmed as he took a step back from Brittany. Searching Ian's face for a moment, Rory saw the moment a lightbulb turned on behind his brother's eyes. "Oh my God! Yeah! Yeah...you're...oh, yeah. I remember you now. You were friends with her. You had big, um—yeah. Yeah. But weren't you a brunette back then?"

Brittany nodded. "Bingo."

"Hallie. Halcyon Gilbert," murmured Ian, more to himself than anyone else. He licked his lips, then bit his bottom lip for a second, deep in thought. All of his flirtatious charm slipped away to show a man affected, maybe even undone, by little more than a name. "Hallie."

"Yeah," said Brittany, her tone dry. "Hallie. Remember

her?"

"Sure. You ever see her?" asked Ian, trying to look cool.

"Once in a while," said Brittany. "We both live in Boston."

Ian cleared his throat. "How's she...how's she doing?"

Brittany took a deep breath. "She's been better, actually."

Ian flinched, his eyes narrowing, his body tensing, his fists clenching by his sides. *Fighting stance*, thought Rory. *Interesting.*

He vaguely remembered Brittany's blonde-haired friend, Halcyon Gilbert, but he had no recollection of Ian and Halcyon being an item. Ian played the field—flagrantly, famously—though it was possible, Rory supposed, that this girl, Hallie, had meant more to him than the others. It was just strange that Ian had never mentioned her, when he had been pretty loud and proud about his conquests back then.

"Why?" demanded Ian. "What happened to her?"

"She's going through a pretty bad divorce," said Brittany, staring at Ian thoughtfully.

Ian's face relaxed. "Sorry to hear that."

Except Rory knew Ian's face like the back of his hand, and Ian's face didn't read "sorry" at all. In fact, it read a little, tiny bit "relieved," like news of Hallie Gilbert's divorce was welcome.

"She has a little girl. Jenny," said Brittany. "It's been a really rough for them."

"Jenny, huh?"

"Yeah. Jenny."

"Well, um...that's too bad. Tell her I say hi, huh?" asked Ian. "If you see her?"

Brittany stared at Ian for a beat before answering, "Umm, no. That's not happening."

"Oh, come on!" said Ian. "She can't still be pissed at me. It's been—what? Ten years?"

Brittany scrunched her lips together, tilting her head left and right as though adding up an equation. "Yeah. Ten years this summer. And still pissed? Oh, you bet. I'm pretty sure you're on her shit list for life, Ian."

From behind Ian, Tierney hooted with laughter, reaching for the sack of biscuits Rory was holding and taking them to the kitchen, muttering something about "Irresistible Ian's not so irresistible now."

Ian, on the other hand, looked at Brittany in surprise for a few minutes before pulling his quilt tighter around his shoulders. "Whatever. I need a shower."

Brittany turned to look at Rory as Ian loped upstairs. "Was I too hard on him?"

Rory shook his head. "You were just right."

"Yeah? I feel a little bad. Like I just kicked a puppy."

"You want the truth? It would have made Ian feel like total crap if you'd treated him with kid gloves."

She chuckled softly, her cheeks coloring. "At A Better Tomorrow, I've learned not to treat the women there like victims. They don't want to be patronized or talked down to."

"You're pretty awesome, Brittany Manion," said Rory, trying desperately to ignore the swelling feeling in his chest that told him *awesome* was just a pallid substitute for all the other words circling in his head: *phenomenal, amazing, epic, enticing, fascinating—*

"Rory? Give me a hand?" called Tierney.

Rory gestured to the couch with a flick of his head. "Make yourself at home. I'll be right back."

He headed into the kitchen, letting the 1940s-style swing door between the living room and kitchen shut behind him. "What?"

"Why in the name of sweet Jaysus did you bring her here?" demanded Tierney, tucking a stray piece of dark hair behind her ear. "And with no notice? I look like a washerwoman from the Liberties!"

"She doesn't care what you look like, one. And two, that was more banter than I've heard out of Ian in years."

"Banter," mumbled Tierney, putting the biscuits on a cookie sheet before popping them in the oven to reheat. "She's Brittany *Manion*, Rory. Mama would have a conniption. What've you got to do with her?"

"She's booking her wedding at Summerhaven."

"What?" Tierney's pinched expression softened, and she reached out to put her hand on Rory's arm. "A wedding! That's great!"

"I know. So can you please be nice?"

Tierney tightened her grip on his arm, her smile fading when she asked, "You say she's getting married?"

"Yes. At Summerhaven, which means I'll have enough money to—"

"You're saying she's *taken*?" interrupted Tierney, her eyes boring into Rory's.

"Generally, an engagement precedes a marriage," said Rory. "Yes. She's taken."

"Well, the way she looks at you says different," said Tierney, letting go of Rory to take four plates out of her cupboard.

"What the hell does that mean?"

"She looks at you like you hung the moon."

"No, she doesn't," said Rory. "She's just...really nice. Kindhearted. I met her yesterday when she came to tour the camp. And then—"

Tierney turned around, her eyes wide, her mouth open. "*She's* the one who took care of the group last night!"

"Can you lower your voice?" asked Rory in an annoyed whisper.

"Am I right?" asked Tierney. "Eh, I know I'm right. She stayed and helped while you were here, didn't she?"

"So what if she did?"

Tierney just stared at him, a very slight smile on her lips.

"She probably looks at everyone like—like they hung the damned moon."

Tierney's mocking smile deepened. "Maybe."

"Anyway," said Rory, "she's headed back to Boston tomorrow, and she'll be getting married at Summerhaven in May. So there's no use in spinning tales in your head, Tierney. She's engaged. She's definitely not interested in me. That's that."

Tierney opened the oven, took out the biscuits and plopped one on each plate before turning back around.

"Whatever you say," she said, then stepped through the swinging door, back into the living room with Brittany.

They'd visited with Ian and Tierney for about an hour before Rory had looked at his watch and said it was time to go.

Although he'd called Chef Jamie to be sure everything was in order for the nine o'clock breakfast, Brittany sensed he wanted to be there to be certain everything went smoothly, especially after missing check-in last night.

Brittany relented and hugged Ian good-bye after he'd begged her for a squeeze. She took Tierney's hand as she left the cottage, thanking her for the biscuit and tea.

She'd enjoyed her visit with the Haven siblings. The conversation was quick, funny, and nonstop. She couldn't remember the last time she'd laughed so hard. One of them was always giving one of the others a hard time, but there was so much love, so much affection and good humor between them, Brittany envied it and wanted to bask in it at the same time.

Her father had remarried to a childless woman who wasn't fond of Brittany (or her massive trust fund), and her mother lived in Tuscany with her much younger boyfriend, Gilles. Brittany hadn't been allowed to build much of a relationship yet with Ben's girls, and while she had some good friends in Boston, those friendships felt polite when contrasted with the boisterous Havens.

Sitting in the car beside Rory, she longed for what he had: family.

But that's why you're marrying Ben, she reminded herself. *You and Ben will build the family you want together. And one day, your children will be like the Havens—giving each other grief but also willing to take a bullet to save the others. You'll have what you want, Brittany. You just have to stay the course.*

"They're a handful," said Rory, as though reading her thoughts.

"I loved visiting with all of you," said Brittany. "I wish

I'd had brothers or sisters."

"You're an only child?" asked Rory. "You know, when I was little, there were times I wished I was an only child." He laughed softly before shaking his head. "Not anymore, though. I love those two. Wouldn't trade them, no matter how much trouble they are."

"Ian looked better after his shower," said Brittany.

"Yeah, he did," agreed Rory, "but his hands were shaking the entire time we were there. I hope he got back in bed when we left."

"I hope he makes it this time."

"Me too," said Rory. He cleared his throat, changing the subject. "So, I want to keep an eye on breakfast and touch base with the housekeeping staff, but once the presentation starts at ten, we can slip out to the florist, okay?"

"Great," said Brittany. "And the photographer too? You mentioned her?"

"Right," murmured Rory, his brow creasing.

I'm starting to recognize that look, thought Brittany. "What's wrong?"

"N-Nothing," said Rory. "I just don't think June's right for your event."

"Is that the photographer's name? June?"

Rory nodded once. "I'll find someone else, okay?"

Hmm. Brittany could sense that something was up with this "June," but Rory didn't seem to want to discuss it, so she didn't press him. "Okay. Thanks. Is there anything I can do to help today?"

"No," said Rory, turning back to her, his eyes unsettled. "Can I ask you something?"

"Go for it."

"Your fiancé…"

"Ben."

"Right. He's older than you are?"

"Mm-hm. He's forty-three."

"Why didn't his first marriage work out?"

Brittany took a deep breath. Did she want to share this with Rory? The answer came quickly: for whatever reason, she did.

"Ben and Angie went to med school together and both worked long hours in the pediatric unit at Mass General. Their first daughter was unplanned, and I don't think they were ready to be parents yet. Between their residencies and Grace, they barely ever saw each other—like ships passing in the night. And then Sabrina came along a few years later. I guess…I mean, I guess they never really got things back on track, and he…"

"He what?"

"He cheated on her."

Rory's neck whipped right to face her. "He *cheated*?"

Brittany gulped at the flinty set of his green eyes. "It was a one-time thing."

"How do you know?"

"Because he told me."

"And you believe him."

Mostly. "Why shouldn't I?"

Rory shifted in his seat, his fingers clenching and unclenching the steering wheel as he took a deep breath and blew it out slowly. "I hope to God you're right."

Me too.

"I am," she said, starting to feel a little bit defensive.

They drove on in awkward silence for a few minutes before Rory spoke again.

"It's just that...you're amazing," he said softly. "You *deserve* amazing."

His words, once again, were like summer rain showering a dry place within her, and she looked over at him now, as she had when he'd called her "gorgeous, smart, and kindhearted," and again when he'd said, "I care more about who *you* are than who you're related to."

You deserve amazing.

How was it that Rory Haven, whom she barely knew, somehow managed to say all of things she so desperately needed to hear? How was it possible that in just a handful of hours, she'd felt more emotionally nourished by his company than she'd felt in a long, long time?

Maybe because so much of the time, she felt ornamental to Ben—like he didn't *see* her, didn't *know* her, and didn't want to expend the time it would take to truly *understand* her heart.

She clasped her fingers together in her lap, her heart racing and chest tightening as these thoughts crystalized in her head for the first time.

Did she and Ben speak the same language? Did they understand each other? Or did they have a communication problem?

Had she chosen to ignore the fact that she and Ben were lacking the emotional intimacy she craved in a partner? Instead of facing the weaknesses in her relationship with Ben, had she chosen to ignore them or gloss over them? Had she chosen to concentrate on the comforting strengths in their relationship—like Ben's financial stability, occupation and role as a doting father—and ignore the fact that sometimes, being with Ben felt lonelier than being alone?

It was frightening to suddenly realize that she was about to marry a man who didn't really know her, especially because she'd convinced herself that she'd chosen Ben for all the right reasons. She didn't *want* to be wrong about him. And she didn't want to have to start all over again with someone new.

She raised her chin, stepping back from the metaphorical cliff and talking herself down.

Ben loved her, and she loved Ben. It's just that they'd both been really busy lately. Maybe Brittany was just feeling some distance from him or the proverbial cold feet that preceded all weddings. Anyway, there were still a few weeks before her wedding—enough time to talk to Ben, to mend whatever wasn't working between them, and get things back on track.

But first and foremost, she needed to get back to Boston. She needed to leave Rory and go back to Ben.

"You know," she said, trying to keep her voice light, "I think I should head back to Boston today, after all."

"What?" said Rory, pulling through the Summerhaven gates before stopping his truck by the side of the road and putting it in park. He turned to her. "No. Wait—Britt, I'm sorry. I shouldn't have asked about Ben's first marriage. I have no right to question you or judge him."

"It's okay," said Brittany, pasting a fake smile on her face. "Really. It doesn't bother me that he made mistakes in the past. I know he loves me, and I know we'll be happy together."

Rory winced. "I can't help feeling I've upset you."

"You haven't," she insisted. "It's been so nice visiting with you, and I definitely want to have my wedding at Summerhaven. If you'll send me a contract, I'll wire the deposit once I'm back in Boston. I'm just…there's so much to do. Guest lists. Invitations. I really should be getting back."

"If you're sure," Rory said softly, sitting back in his seat, clenching his jaw as he stared out the windshield.

"I am. But I'll compare calendars with Ben and arrange a time to come back, okay? We can do the tasting then and visit the florist. And if you could get a new recommendation for a photographer, that would be great."

"Whatever you need," he said, his voice flat and low.

They rode the rest of the way to the office in silence and said a formal good-bye, shaking hands briefly before Brittany got back into her car and drove away.

chapter eight

"A camp?" asked Ben, wrinkling his nose over shrimp linguine. "Two hours away?"

"You wanted me to plan everything, right?" asked Brittany, spinning her fork around in her bowl. It had been a long time since she'd eaten something as carb-loaded as pasta, but she was in the mood for it tonight, so she'd ordered takeout from her favorite Italian restaurant.

"Right, but I also asked you to keep it simple. I mean, I was thinking a justice of the peace with a few close friends and some lunch afterward."

"Well, then," she said, taking a sip of wine, "maybe you should have said that."

"I *did* say it," he replied, looking up at her in annoyance. "I *said* I wanted simple."

She thought about addressing their communication issues here and now, but Ben had only arrived twenty minutes ago and spent the first ten minutes griping about how pasta meant he'd need to put in an extra thirty minutes at the gym tomorrow. She didn't think it was the right time to open the can of worms labeled "Communication."

She sighed, reaching across the table for his hand and weaving her fingers through his. "Ben, I love it up there. So much. I spent four of the happiest summers of my life on that lake, and I just thought that it would be a great place for us to get away with our friends and loved ones for a weekend. You said we wouldn't have time for a honeymoon until the fall, but if we stayed at Summerhaven for a couple of nights, it would be like having the wedding and honeymoon up there at the same time."

Ben squeezed her hand before pulling his away. "Two hours is going to be inconvenient for a lot of people."

"It means a lot to me."

He shrugged. "Fine. Whatever you want."

"It's really beautiful. Cottages. A lake. A ropes course! I bet the girls love it. Speaking of the girls…" She waited to see if he'd offer up any information about his time with his daughters yesterday. When he didn't, she gave him a nudge. "How did yesterday go? How did the girls feel about a Memorial Day weekend wedding?"

"Oh," he said, wiping his mouth. "I haven't mentioned it to them yet."

"What? Ben, you promised. That's why you told me I couldn't join you."

"I know, babe," he said. "But plans got changed around at the last minute, and it didn't feel right to bring it up."

"Feel *right*? What do you mean?"

Ben sighed, blowing out a big puff of air as he picked up his wineglass. "When the girls picked me up on Sunday morning, it just happened that Angie was getting off her shift at the same time. So, there I was, and there she was, and the girls invited her to join us."

Brittany sat back in her chair, staring at him in shock. "Are you saying that you, Angie, and the girls spent the whole day together?"

He rolled his eyes before taking a sip of wine. "I *knew* you'd overreact."

"Am I overreacting? I'm just asking a question for clarification, Ben."

"Yes. I spent the day with my daughters and their mother," he said, his voice annoyed. "We had some lunch, shopped for summer clothes for the girls, got some ice cream…"

"What else?" Brittany whispered, her heart clenching at the happy-family visions in her head.

Ben exhaled a long-suffering sigh, like Brittany was torturing him for her own pleasure. "We went back to Angie's and I grilled some steaks for dinner while the girls took a swim, and then Sabrina wanted to watch a movie."

"So you stayed?"

"Of course. Why would I say no? We watched *Vacation* because it was always one of our favorites." He shrugged, taking another sip of wine. "Nothing *happened*, Brittany. It was no big deal. Just some standard family time."

Family time.

He threw the words away like they didn't mean anything, though they made her breath catch with longing. She imagined the four of them lined up on a couch together, big bowls of popcorn on their laps and barely room for a breath between them.

"Family time," she repeated, blinking against an onslaught of hot tears, which was strange because the last time she'd experienced "family time" on Saturday morning with the Havens, she'd felt envy, but not the stark, cold, terrible sadness she felt now.

"I have no idea why this is such an issue for you,

Brittany, but it's really getting old."

His words made her angry, which made her tears recede a little. "You can't figure out why it bothers me that you, *my fiancé*, spent a cozy day with Angie, *your ex-wife*?"

"Nothing *happened*," he repeated, his eyes flashing with anger as he stood up to uncork another bottle of wine. "I thought you were trying harder to understand. She's the mother of my girls, Brittany. She'll always be a part of my family."

"Your family? No, Ben. She'll always be a part of your life, maybe, but she's not your family anymore. You got *divorced*, remember?"

"Yeah. I remember," he growled softly, leveling her with his eyes from where he stood at the kitchen counter. "But that's where you're wrong. She's still family. Always will be."

"Damn it!" cried Brittany, throwing her napkin on the table. "Can't you understand how that makes me feel? I mean, you and I are getting married. *Married*, Ben. *I'm* supposed to be your family, not Angie."

"Jesus!" He ran a hand through his hair before picking up the open wine bottle and bringing it to the table. "This isn't just about *you*, Brittany. You're going to have to make room for Angie."

"And if I don't?"

Slowly, he poured his glass to the rim, picked it up, took a sip, then looked at her. "Frankly? If the mother of my children is going to be a problem for you, then maybe—I don't know, babe—maybe we're moving too fast here."

All of the oxygen in the room was sucked into the great beyond, and Brittany could barely breathe. "W-What? What does *that* mean?"

"It means that maybe we should put wedding plans on hold and slow down a little…maybe you need a little time to get your head around everything."

"Around *what*? You having cozy family dinners with your ex while I'm told not to join you? I'm never going to get my head around that, Ben!"

Ben placed his glass back down on the table, crossing his arms over his chest. "She's going to be at their graduations. At their weddings. God willing, someday we'll have grandchildren together, me and Angie. Do you know how good yesterday was for our girls? Do you have any idea?" He paused, staring blankly at the half-finished bowl of pasta on the table in front of him. "It's been *years* since she gave me the time of day, Brittany. Years since she didn't look at me like garbage. This is a *good* thing. Believe me."

"For who?" asked Brittany, her voice breaking.

"For all of us. The girls. Angie. Me." He paused, then looked up at her quickly. "And you too. You're too jealous to see it now, but it'll be good for everyone if Angie and I are friends."

Is that what you are? Friends? After being each other's first loves? First spouses? After sharing the highs and lows of parenthood? After the painful way that your marriage ended? Because if you were only friends, I could handle this. But I don't see how two people who have shared what you and Angie have shared can ever just be friends.

All of these questions and thoughts circled in her head wildly, but in the end, she didn't ask them. Maybe because she couldn't bear the answers she might see in his eyes.

"I'm just not comfortable with it," she whispered, raising her eyes to his face.

Ben sighed, grimacing as he picked up his plate and hers. He put both in the sink, then turned to face her, leaning against the kitchen counter. "Well, I hope you can figure out how to *get* comfortable, babe. Because Angie's not going anywhere."

"So, whether I like it or not, Angie's in the picture," she said.

Ben nodded, then rolled away from the counter and headed toward the bathroom in the back hall.

Brittany had been holding back her tears, but now they slipped down her cheeks in streams.

The thing was? Brittany didn't want Angie totally *out* of the picture. She understood that Angie was Grace and Sabrina's mother. She respected Angie's place and position in Ben's history and in the girls' present and future. Brittany would never want for those two girls to be deprived of their mother. She *wanted* Ben and Angie on civil terms. Hell, she'd like to be on civil terms with Angie too. But Brittany wanted to be Ben's *priority*—she didn't want to feel like she was competing with Angie for Ben's attention. For the past couple of weeks? She did. And it hurt.

Wiping away her tears, she picked up her wineglass and stood up from the table. Suddenly Ben was behind her, his arms around her. She was stiff against him, but he nuzzled her neck, his fingers slipping under her blouse to knead the tender skin under her breasts.

"Come on, beautiful," he said. "Let's go to bed. We can hash this out in the morning."

But if Brittany didn't insist on what she wanted now, how could she fault Ben for giving her less than what she needed later? She either needed to fix what was wrong in their relationship…or—and it broke her heart to admit this to herself—she had to face the fact that maybe she and Ben just weren't right for each other. Either way, she was too emotional to do either tonight.

"I'm really tired," she said.

"Fine," he said, a twinge of disappointment in his voice. "We'll just go to sleep."

"You know," said Brittany, untangling herself from his arms, then turning to face him, "I think I'd rather be alone tonight."

"What?" His head whipped back like she'd smacked him, his eyes searching hers with disbelief. "Are you serious?"

She nodded. "You said I needed time to get my head around things, right?"

Ben crossed his arms over his chest, clearly irritated that she was throwing his words back at him. "You're acting like a brat."

She crossed her arms over her own chest and didn't reply, staring back at him, willing him to leave so that she could cry in peace and try to figure out if sharing Ben with Angie was something she could accept in her future—a future that looked less clear and more confusing every day lately.

"Grow up," he said curtly. "Call me when you're ready to be an adult."

He grabbed his keys and jacket off the counter and slammed the front door shut as he left.

And Brittany stood frozen in the quiet of her kitchen, too shocked to cry, hugging her body tightly like it had just taken a beating.

It's a terrible thing, thought Rory, who rose at dawn after another fitful night of crappy sleep, *when your mind seizes on someone and won't let go.*

A week had passed since Britt had driven away from Summerhaven, but she was constantly on his mind. He rewound their conversations in his head, thinking about her, wondering about her, undone by her beauty, but even more captivated by her goodness.

He liked the way she blurted out things like "Breeding?" or "Do bears poop in the woods?" He liked the way she'd jumped in to help him last Friday night, expecting nothing in return. He liked the way she gave Ian a hard time but still hugged him good-bye. And he especially liked the way she looked curled up on the couch in his living room when he came home on Friday night. That was the image his brain most loved to conjure, even though it caused a painful longing that only stopped when he reminded himself of her impending nuptials.

He didn't know her fiancé personally, of course, but Rory felt sick when he thought of "Dr. Douche" and the few unsavory things about him: he made Brittany feel self-conscious about her weight, he didn't have any interest in learning to ski even though she loved it, and—worst of all—he'd cheated on his first wife. Any one of these things on its own might have bothered Rory, but added up? He didn't care if this guy was a great doctor or a good dad to his daughters; he simply wasn't good enough for Brittany.

Not that it mattered.

Britt had e-mailed him on Sunday, thanking him for showing her around and reminding him to send her a contract. He'd sent her the agreement via e-mail and she'd signed it and sent it back right away, along with a $10,000 deposit. He wrote back asking when she'd like to come back for a tasting, but his e-mail hadn't been answered yet, and he was positive because he'd probably checked his inbox a hundred times.

Pulling on jeans and a flannel shirt, he padded down the hallway to the kitchen, grabbing an energy bar, which he gnawed on while he pulled on socks and boots. Then he headed downstairs, through the dark, quiet office, to the ax and stump behind the office.

Every morning this week, he'd gotten up around five, after dreams of Brittany Manion woke him in a state of painful arousal, and expended that leftover energy chopping firewood.

He placed a log on the stump, raised the ax, and *thwack*!—the satisfying noise of splitting wood followed.

"She's getting married," he grunted, picking up half the split log and halving it again.

"And besides, she's out of your league, man. *Way* out of your league."

Another *thwack*, another set of twin logs. He carried all four to the pile against the back of the building, then placed a new log on the stump.

"She's a gorgeous, rich, sophisticated woman. You run a camp-slash-conference center in the middle of nowhere."

Thwack.

A bead of sweat slipped down the side of his face.

"Not to mention, you and Britt are a serious conflict of

interest. She's an heiress with megahospitality connections, and you're in need of capital to franchise your conference center idea. She's already worried people will only want to be with her for her money and connections. She'd be suspicious of you from the get-go. She'd always wonder if you were with her for the right reasons or for what she could do for you." He took another armload of logs to the pile, wiping the sweat from his brow with the sleeve of his shirt. "Nah, man. Even if she was free, there's no way it could work unless you gave up your dream."

Another log landed with a *thud* on the chopping stump, and the ax fell twice with the power needed to split it. Rory grunted with satisfaction when the halves went flying in opposite directions.

Out of nowhere, he thought of her hips beneath his hands when he'd moved her aside, on a search for Tierney's slippers. Just a little bit of softness, though he wouldn't mind more if she wanted her carbs back. And as he'd sidestepped passed her, she'd smelled like sweet, warm woman—like bed, like heaven.

"Fuck!" he yelled, bringing the ax down again.

He needed to deal with this.

Pulling his phone from his hip pocket, he opened his messenger app and typed "June." When her number came up, he messaged: *What are you up to tonight? Want some company?*

He leaned on the ax, staring at the screen, knowing that she was probably awake. June often got up early to photograph the sunrise, then slept for a few hours during the day before getting up again in the late afternoon.

JUNE: Just thinking about you, lover. Did you catch the rays on the lake just now?

RORY: Missed them.
JUNE: Your loss. Spectacular.
RORY: Tonight?
JUNE: You're an eager beaver.
RORY: Haven't seen you in a while.
JUNE: I got back from Denver yesterday.

Rory stared at his phone, waiting for her to say yes or no.

JUNE: Sure. Tonight's good. 8?
RORY: It's a date.
JUNE: No, it's a fuck. But you're cute. xo

Generally, Rory got a rush when June talked dirty. He liked it that he called their lovemaking "fucking" because, honestly, that's exactly what it was: no-strings-attached sex. But today, the words just washed over him like noise, adding to his restlessness.

He spent the remainder of the day in a foul mood, avoiding Mrs. Toffle, Chef Jamie, and his assistant manager, Doug, who returned to work today and to whom Rory had assigned linen and towel inventory in preparation for the busy summer season.

They had specialty camps and conferences booked every week from June 4 through September 14 and would make more than 80 percent of their annual profits during those crucial fifteen weeks. Summerhaven needed to be a well-oiled machine to maintain its excellent reputation.

At seven thirty, Rory showered and shaved, putting on clean jeans and a fresh polo shirt, then stopped at the Holderness Market for a bouquet of flowers and six-pack of June's favorite IPA.

"Right on time," she purred, opening the screen door

for him as Rory walked from his truck to her lakeside cottage.

June lived on the other side of the lake in a house she'd inherited from her grandparents and fixed up with money she'd earned as an AP photographer in her twenties and thirties. All over June's cottage were framed pictures of faraway places—Egypt, Thailand, Bolivia, Antarctica—interspersed around dusty trophies she'd won over the years.

"Hey," he said, surprised by the sharp stab of disappointment he felt as he drew closer to June. He forced a smile. "How was Denver?"

"Good late-season powder," said June, raising one eyebrow. "How was Sandwich?"

"Same old," said Rory, leaning forward to kiss her cheek.

He leaned back and offered her the flowers and beer.

"You're adorable," she said, taking them from him with a smile. "Like an old-fashioned suitor coming to call on his lady friend." She leaned in and whispered, "Except we both know I'm not a lady."

She walked to the kitchen, her tinkling anklet harmonizing with her low chuckle, her long multicolored skirt swirling at her feet.

"You want one?" she asked, pulling two beers from the cardboard box and holding them up.

"Sure," said Rory.

As June opened their drinks, Rory gazed out at the lake, trying to get his head in the game. He was here with June. June, who'd traveled the globe and learned a thing or two about pleasing a man. June, who offered comfort and pleasure with zero expectations. June, who was every single guy's dream.

She sauntered over, holding out his bottle. They clinked them together, then sipped, June grinning at him over the rim of hers.

"So? What's up with you? You seem…out of sorts today."

Rory stepped into her screened porch, which was warm from an electric heater oscillating in the corner of the room. He sat down on the worn couch, and June sat down beside him.

"I don't know," he said. "I'm…" He sighed. "I don't know."

"Sure you do," said June, tucking her feet under her bottom and pulling a blanket from the back of the couch. "And I wager my forty-four years on your twenty-seven that you'll feel a lot better if you spit it out."

June might be right, but Rory wasn't going to show up at her house, primarily for sexual release, only to start off the night talking about Brittany.

"Stupid stuff."

"Oh, come on now. Girls aren't stupid," said June, as though reading his mind. "In my experience, boys are *far* stupider."

"True, that. I barely know her *and* she's engaged," he blurted out. "You're exactly right. I'm stupid and she's impossible."

"Ah-ha," said June, nodding sagely before she took another sip of beer.

"Honestly, I'm not even that interested in her."

June's hand landed in his lap, her fingers on his crotch, but Rory gently pulled them away.

"All evidence to the contrary," said June.

Rory held her hand, lifting it to his lips and kissing the back gently before letting go. "I shouldn't have come over tonight, June. I'm sorry."

"I'm not," she said, placing her beer on the coffee table, then taking his and doing the same. "We can still fuck. I don't mind."

"You don't mind that I'm thinking about someone else?"

"No. Why would I mind? It might even make things hotter." She laughed for a moment, then stopped, scanning his eyes before sobering to explain, "Whether you're thinking about her or me, your cock's long and thick, and when you slide into me, lover, it's all mine. You lap up my cunt like it's covered in honey, and you make that sexy fucking sound in the back of your throat when you come. Why would I care who you're thinking about? You're a damn good fuck, Rory. Our arrangement isn't exclusive, and I'm not looking to change that. It's perfect the way it is."

Except…it wasn't. Not for Rory. Not anymore.

Because despite the hot things she'd just said about him, there was no part of Rory that wanted to have sex with June. Have a beer? Sure. Sit and talk? Absolutely. But get naked? He couldn't think of anything he wanted less. He didn't want to fuck June or anyone else. The only woman he could think about was Brittany.

"Oh, dear," said June, leaning forward to pick up her beer. "She's not just anyone, is she?"

"No," murmured Rory, hating that it was true. "She's not just anyone."

"I think you've got it bad, lover," said June.

I think you're right.

"Well, I tell you what…why don't we finish our drinks and call it a night? I have pictures to edit, and you, my sweet, are clearly not in the mood for fucking."

Rory winced, turning to June apologetically. "Sorry."

"Don't be," she said, smiling at him. "If your impossible girl stays impossible, you'll have to let her go, won't you? When you do, give me a call. I'll be here."

June's tone held a slight note of mockery, and Rory turned to her. "She *is* impossible, June. She's getting married to someone else."

"I know what engaged means," she said lightly. "It means 'not married yet.'"

"It means 'not available.'"

"Take my advice, darling: either put up your dukes or move along." She tilted her head to the side. "Me? I'm not a fighter by nature. Never was, never will be. That's probably why I never fell in love. Love is the biggest battle there is."

Rory stared at her, confused by this point of view. He'd always regarded love as something that just happened—you fell into love, right? Slipped into it. Stumbled upon it. Felt it suddenly bubble up within you, unexpectedly, and maybe unwanted. Love and fate were bound together, mysterious and inextricable.

But June was suggesting that an engaged woman was still available—no, it wouldn't be easy to win her—that with enough "fight," Brittany could somehow be his? He didn't even know where to start or how to begin. For heaven's sake, this morning he'd convinced himself of all the reasons he and Brittany *wouldn't* work.

Besides, the fact remained that she was getting *married*

in a few weeks.

"How do you fight for someone who's already been won by someone else?" he murmured, the question an extension of his swirling, confusing thoughts.

"Oh, Rory, my sweet Boy Scout." June hummed softly, finishing the last of her beer before meeting Rory's eyes. "You break the rules."

CHAPTER NINE

The Monday after their fight, Brittany still hadn't called Ben, nor had he reached out to her.

At first, when her hurt and indignation were sharpest, she'd expected a grand gesture, like a bouquet of flowers with an apology or a knock on her door to reveal a complacent Ben, holding a bottle of chilled champagne and two crystal flutes.

By three of four days after, her expectations had lessened—she hoped for a conciliatory phone call or a sweet text telling her that he missed her and wanted to work things out.

By the end of the week, Brittany had to face the fact that she must have been in the wrong because his silence told her that no apology was forthcoming. If she wanted to get things back on track with Ben, she'd need to make the first move. She *was* the one who'd thrown him out, after all.

After a week of thinking, she'd decided that she could make room for Angie in her life with Ben. As long as he prioritized *her* over his ex-wife, there would be room for everyone. Brittany just needed to trust Ben. He deserved that, didn't he? He'd never given her a reason to question his commitment to her. And he was right—if he got along with Angie, it was better for everyone, especially the girls. And

Brittany only wanted the very best for Ben's daughters.

On Tuesday morning, she called Ben's receptionist and asked what hours he'd be working. Told that he'd be in the Mass General ER for most of the day, Brittany pulled on big-girl panties, Ben's favorite jeans (which fit especially well, as she'd been starving herself since pasta night), and a cream cashmere sweater. Paired with pearls and metallic gold flats, she looked sophisticated but cute and felt confident as she hailed a cab in Cambridge around noon. She directed the cabbie to the hospital, hoping to talk to Ben in person during his lunch break.

Striding through the automatic doors, she stopped at the information desk and said hello to Cecilia, the receptionist, who double-checked Ben's schedule and confirmed that he'd be coming up for a break in about fifteen minutes. She thanked Cecilia, then headed to the elevators, pressing the button for the fourth floor, where the cafeteria was located. Choosing a small table in the sun beside the floor-to-ceiling windows, she withdrew a bud vase and a single white rose from her purse—white for surrender—then took a seat at the table, facing the cafeteria entrance, and waited for Ben to appear.

It wasn't long before she saw him—his blond, salt-and-pepper head inclined to the woman he was talking with as he entered the cafeteria. His eyes crinkled with humor, animated and soft, his body tilted toward her as they stood in line for trays. She was tiny and brunette, similarly dressed in light-blue scrubs and a white lab coat, and totally captivating when she flashed Ben a megawatt smile.

Angela.

Though they'd never met in person, Brittany had met

Ben's petite, olive-skinned, dark-haired daughters a couple of times, and they were doppelgängers of their mother.

This *must* be Angie.

Observing her nemesis from where she sat by the windows, Brittany noted that Angie was much smaller and slimmer than she, with her dark hair wound up in a chic bun. She wore dark-rimmed glasses that made her look super smart, her cheekbones were high, and her lips were red and full. She was a tiny, gorgeous, brilliant Italian American goddess-doctor, and Brittany felt useless, fat, and lumpy just looking at her.

She dropped her eyes to her engagement ring, watching it sparkle in the sun, and took a deep breath, reminding herself that Ben wasn't married to Angie anymore. He was, in fact, engaged to her.

Standing, she put her Louis Vuitton bag on her arm, squared her shoulders, and approached Ben and Angie from behind, picking up snippets of their conversation as she drew closer.

"She was always a stinker, Benji! You know that!"

"I know, I know. But she's almost fifteen now. I was certain she'd grow out of that."

"Fat chance," said Angie, placing a hand on his arm. "She's her father's daughter."

"Maybe, Ang. But she got her mother's looks, thank God."

"Ah-hem," said Brittany, clearing her throat. "Ben?"

He turned around so quickly, his tray rammed into her stomach, causing a full mug of coffee to splash on her cream sweater.

"W-What? Brittany?"

"God!" she cried, gasping as the hot liquid burned her skin. She pulled the fabric away from her stomach, fanning it as droplets off coffee fell on her shoes, dulling the gold shimmer.

"Aw, shit!" he exclaimed, looking at the spreading brown spot. "Are you okay? Sorry."

Brittany looked up and blinked at him. "I'm fine. No worries."

"You surprised me. W-What are you doing here?"

The woman behind Ben in line offered Brittany a handful of napkins, and she blotted her now cooling sweater. "I um, well…that was the point. A surprise. I thought I'd surprise you for lunch."

"You, uh…" He looked at Angie, and Brittany followed his glance, meeting Angie's wide brown eyes behind those fashionable glasses. "You should have texted so I knew you were coming."

She ignored Ben, offering Angie the hand that wasn't covered in coffee. "Hi. You must be Angie. I'm Brittany."

Angie didn't make a move to set down her tray. Nor did she smile, though she did manage a curt nod as she said, "Hi."

Brittany awkwardly lowered her hand. "I've heard a lot about you."

"Is that right?" asked Angie, flicking a look at Ben before sliding her eyes back to his fiancé.

"Yes," Brittany said, trying to keep her voice warm. "I hear you're a wonderful mother."

"Hmm," Angie hummed, blinking at Brittany, unsmiling. "Do you have any children, Bethany?"

"It's Brittany. And, um, no. Not yet." As she said this,

she looked up at Ben, who couldn't possibly look more uncomfortable than he did right now.

"Yet?" asked Angie, looking at Ben for a long moment before turning back to Brittany with a sigh. "But you want them?"

"Of course."

"Are you planning to adopt?"

"No," said Brittany, wondering why Angie would ask such a question. Perhaps she didn't want Ben to have more biological children to compete with hers? "My own."

"Well…that'll be quite the trick," said Angie with a grim smile. She turned to Ben. "You need to talk to her. Catch you later?"

"Yeah," said Ben, watching as Angie turned away from them, headed to the food station across the room.

Brittany's cheeks flared from the awkward meeting, but she was most bothered by Angie's questions.

"Ben? What was that all about?"

"What?"

"'Quite the trick.' What did she mean by that?"

"Nothing."

"Ben," she insisted, annoyed that he was still tracking Angie's progress at the goddamned salad bar, where she was piling up on lettuce and carrots with no dressing. Brittany was getting upset, her fingers cold and shaky, like something terrible was about to happen. "Please tell me what she meant."

"We need to talk." Sighing, Ben placed his tray on a counter, and took her arm. "Come with me."

He walked briskly to a waiting room just outside the cafeteria, pulling her inside and closing the door. Once alone, he faced her, staring down at her face.

"It's reversible."

"What is?"

"A vasectomy."

A vasectomy?

She couldn't breathe. She couldn't breathe. It felt like her throat was closing up. Ben whacked her on the back and she suddenly inhaled, sharply, painfully.

"Calm down, Brittany."

"You c-can't—you can't have kids?"

He stared at her, then sighed, shaking his head.

"W-When did you have it? The...v-vasectomy?"

"After Sabrina was born."

The room was spinning like a cyclone, all of her hopes and dreams swirling into a big black funnel. She'd chosen him because he was a great dad, because he loved kids, because surely he wanted more kids, because he knew how terribly she wanted children of her own.

"But you knew...you knew how much I...you knew I wanted..." She couldn't form sentences, couldn't find the words she needed in her muddled head.

"Brittany," he said, putting his hands on her shoulders and shaking her gently, "calm down. Just breathe."

She reached up for his hands, pulling them from her shoulders, then took two steps back until her thighs bumped into an aqua, vinyl-covered loveseat. Slowly, she lowered herself down, her fingers curling into the plastic on either side of her hips.

"Why didn't you tell me?" she whispered.

"For one, you never asked—"

"*If you'd had a vasectomy?*" she half-sobbed, half-screamed. "Ben! Why would I ask that? And why the hell would you get involved with me if you didn't want any more kids? The night you met me, I was *sobbing* over the fact that my ex-husband had started a family with another woman! I didn't *have* to ask. You *knew*!"

"I didn't know if I wanted more kids!" he bellowed. "I just wanted to be with you! You were fun and young…and things were so hot between us. I fell for you. You made me forget about my divorce and—and…and things just…"

"Things just *what*?" she asked, her voice far away like she was having an out-of-body experience.

"Got serious! You'd look at me with those wide eyes, wanting more, needing more, and I wanted to be there for you. I like you, Brittany. So much, and I—"

"You *like* me?" she demanded, her voice breaking off at a high-pitched shriek. "I'm going to be your *wife*!"

Her words seemed to reverberate off the walls like a grotesque echo: *Wife. Wife. Wife.* Ben didn't say anything. Tight-lipped, his expression a mix of annoyance and contrition, he shook his head and whispered, "I don't think so."

"Oh. My. God." Her whole body slumped and hot tears pricked the back of her eyes. "Are you breaking off our engagement?"

"You knew this was coming. You knew something was off between us."

It was another blow, because she knew that things weren't perfect between them, but no, she hadn't seen this coming. Certainly not today when she had picked up a white rose on the way to lunch.

"*Fuck you, Ben*! I paid the deposit on our wedding venue

five days ago! We're getting married in six weeks!"

"I didn't give you that date! You *forced* it on me!"

She gasped in shock. "I didn't force you to propose six months ago."

He ran his hands through his hair. "But you did, babe. I knew it was what you wanted."

"What did *you* want?" she murmured.

"*Please* make this easier for me," he begged her in a gravelly voice.

Her eyes flared with indignation and anger. "For *you*? Easier for *you*?"

She jumped to her feet, beating at his chest with balled fists, tears streaming down her face as she sobbed that she hated him and he was a cheating asshole and why did he propose if he never loved her? If he never meant to marry her in the first place?

Holding her wrists tightly, he looked down at her face, his own eyes watery. "I *did* love you. I *did* mean to marry you. But then…but then…"

He looked at her helplessly, and suddenly, in a flash, she knew. She knew why she'd objected more and more to Angie—because no matter how much she wanted to deny what was wrong between her and Ben, she couldn't fool her intuition.

"Angie," she sobbed. "You stopped w-wanting to be w-with me because Angie d-decided to f-forgive you."

Ben nodded, reaching up to brush a stray tear into his hairline. "Yeah."

"You still"—she gulped—"love her."

"Yeah."

"You want her back."

"Yeah." He nodded, letting go of her other wrist and backing into a chair. He sat down, leaning forward, resting his elbows on his knees and rubbing his cheeks. "It's what she wants too."

You need to talk to her. Catch you later?

"Oh. Oh, my God, I'm such an idiot." Brittany sat back down on the loveseat, feeling spent and foolish. "Did you sleep with her?" When Ben didn't answer, Brittany looked up at him. The answer was written on his face, but she needed to hear the words anyway. "Did you?"

"Not until this week," he said, staring down at the floor. "Not until you threw me out on Monday."

"Oh, wow," she said, laughing at him bitterly through her tears. "So it's *my* fault that you fucked your ex-wife while you were engaged to me?"

His neck jerked up when she cursed because she didn't do it all that often. He shrugged, looking miserable. "I didn't say that."

"Is anything ever *your* fault, Ben?"

Raising her hand from where it was fisted on the plastic upholstery, she unfurled her fingers, looking down at the diamond ring he'd given her. It didn't sparkle in this dimly lit waiting room as it had at the table beside the windows. Her tears stopped as she slid it off her finger. She stood up, crossed the room, pulled Ben's hand from his knee, turned it over, and placed the ring in his palm.

He closed his fingers over the ring, looking up at her.

"I'm sorry, Brittany. I'm really sorry."

And suddenly, looking down at his face, she realized something important: she wasn't.

Oh, she was sorry that he wasn't the man she thought

he was, and she was sorry that her plans to start a family would be delayed. She was sorry that she hadn't seen the signs sooner, and she was sorry that she'd wasted more than a year of her life with him.

But she wasn't sorry to be walking away from this user, this cheater, this man who would have eventually broken her heart if she'd stayed with him.

There was even the tiniest part of her that was grateful. Not to him, but to the fates or grace or the universe for showing her exactly who he was before it was too late.

She lifted her chin and straightened her spine.

"I'm not," she said simply.

Then she turned on her heel, put her back to Dr. Benjamin Parker, and walked away.

Rory found that doing improvements around Summerhaven—hard, manual labor—was one of the best ways to shut down his thoughts of Brittany Manion. And though he hadn't been this impacted by a woman in a long time, he had to admit that little by little, day by day, his feelings for her softened and faded.

He hadn't seen or heard from her in a week in a half, though he still held her deposit. No doubt she was busy back in Boston, making plans for her wedding. And though part of his heart still clenched at the thought of her, Rory had mostly made his peace with the fact that Brittany couldn't be the girl for him.

That said, meeting her and becoming infatuated with her had shifted some things in Rory's head. He could see himself spending his life with someone like Brittany—having a slew of kids and living happily ever after. Up until now, Rory hadn't thought much about the sort of woman he wanted to marry—hell, even though his parents' marriage had been strong and sound, Rory hadn't really thought much about a wife at all. But now he found he couldn't shake the thought of finding someone like Brittany and settling down—finding her on the couch in front of the fire every day after work, taking walks around the Summerhaven campus in the fall, skinny-dipping in the lake on hot summer nights, and—he always smiled when he thought of their conversation—breeding. Oh, yeah. Lots and lots of breeding.

"Hand me some more nails?" muttered Ian.

As his hot daydreams scattered, Rory reached over to the plastic cup holding nails and grabbed a handful for Ian, taking a look at his brother as he passed them over.

Squatting on the cottage roof with the sunlight on his black hair, Ian looked so much better than he had when he arrived on Tierney's doorstep, but he still had a long road of recovery ahead.

He'd put on weight over the past two weeks because Tierney was spoiling him with their mother's Irish specialties every night. And days like this one—spent in the sun making repairs on cottages or cleaning up and mulching the various Summerhaven gardens—put some healthy color on Ian's face. His hair was back in a ponytail and his jaw was still covered with a thick black beard, but his eyes were clear.

He was attending the AA meetings in Sandwich, Holderness, and Moultonborough religiously, and Rory knew he hadn't had a drop of drink since he'd arrived at

Tierney's. But he still worried. These were the most tenuous days of recovery, and Ian still needed all the support he could get.

"You look good, Ian," said Rory, pushing a roof shingle into place and securing it with nails.

"I feel like climbing the walls," he grunted.

"We knew it wouldn't be easy."

"*We?*" demanded Ian, nailing another shingle to the roof. "Are you the one in AA? Are you the one whose life is shit?"

This was a common thread among recovery alcoholics: self-pity, or the feeling that life was shit and couldn't be fun, couldn't be enjoyable, without alcohol. Rory knew from everything he'd read that it would take a while for Ian to achieve actual sobriety, wherein he was not only abstinent from alcohol but also found meaning and purpose in life without it.

"It's a process, Ian."

"Yeah. It's a fucking process, all right."

"Mr. Haven? Mr. Haven? Oh, Lord, is this working? Mr. H—"

Rory unclipped the walkie-talkie from his waist. "Hey, Mrs. T. You looking for me?"

"Oh! There you are. Over."

From beside him, Rory heard the unexpected sound of Ian chuckling—a gritty sound, like that of a machine that hasn't been turned on in a while, all rusty cogs and unoiled gears. "I forgot she did that."

Rory grinned. Thank goodness for Miranda Toffle for adding a little levity.

"What's up, Mrs. Toffle?"

"There's a guest here without a reservation, looking for a place to take a retreat. Hoping to stay in one of the Oxford Row cabins for a few weeks. Over."

Unscheduled guests at Summerhaven were pretty unusual, though not unheard of. "Well, we're working on Trinity now, and we've got Kellogg, St. Anne, and Pembroke scheduled for maintenance this week and next."

There was a slight pause before Mrs. Toffle asked, "How about Lady Margaret? Over."

"All done," said Rory. He and Ian had finished all maintenance issues on Lady Margaret earlier in the week.

"So, it's available? Over."

"For how long, Mrs. Toffle? We have the Manion wedding over Memorial Day weekend, and I still don't have a headcount. We might need it."

"I'll ask. Over." A few seconds passed before Mrs. Toffle returned. While he waited, Rory looked out at the lake. From his vantage point on top of Trinity, it sparkled like diamonds in the spring sunshine.

"That's no problem. She'll just rent it for six weeks. Over."

She. Hmm. For just a second, he wondered about this "she." Perhaps it was fate that a fresh face would arrive on campus for an extended stay just when Rory had decided that he was interested in meeting someone new.

"Mrs. T, can you be sure she understands that it's $200 a day? That's…" He did the math quickly in his head. "That's $8,400. Close to $10,000 after state tax."

"Hold, please. Over." A minute later, she was back on the line. "That's fine. Over."

"Okay, then. Write up a contract and take a deposit,

please."

"All set," said Mrs. Toffle. "I'll bring her down in a golf cart as soon as we're sorted. Over and out."

Rory clipped his walkie-talkie back on his belt loop and looked over at Ian. "Someone wants to rent Lady Margaret for the next six weeks. Some kind of retreat."

Ian nodded. "Probably a writer."

"Or an artist."

"Or a photographer," said Ian, giving his brother shit about June.

"Or a super limber yoga instructor," said Rory, raising an eyebrow.

"Oh, God, *please*," said Ian, cracking a rare smile.

Rory chuckled, reaching for his T-shirt and putting it on as he stepped over to the ladder at the edge of the roof. He could hear the golf cart approaching and ran a hand through his hair after he climbed down. He probably looked like hell after sweating on the roof all morning, but hopefully their new guest would be the understanding type.

As Mrs. Toffle came into view, driving at approximately three miles per hour, Rory felt his whole body freeze as his mouth dropped open. There, beside Mrs. T, wearing sunglasses, with her beautiful blonde hair in a ponytail, was Brittany Manion.

A fire lit in his chest, sparks alighting inside of him, heating his blood with barely restrained want. And every feeling Rory had been fighting against, every thought he'd tried to shelve, every stupid hope he'd almost given up on came rushing back, whirling into his heart like a tornado and displacing everything else there before.

Britt was back.

He felt his smile grow until it had spread from ear to ear, his eyes focused like lasers on her face as the golf cart rumbled to a slow stop in front of Lady Margaret, two cabins down from Trinity.

"Britt!" he exclaimed, offering her his hand to help her form the cart and telling himself that he didn't know her well enough to draw her into his arms, no matter how much he wanted to. "Welcome back! I had no idea you were coming! You should have…"

His voice trailed off as he looked closer at her. She didn't offer him a smile and pulled her hand away pretty quickly once her feet were firmly on the ground. Suddenly Rory wished he could see her eyes.

"Hi, Rory," she murmured.

"Hey," he said, taking a step back from her, still scanning her face, trying to figure out what was wrong. Was she thinner than she'd been two weeks ago or was it just his imagination? No. She was definitely thinner. What was she doing here? And—*Oh my God*—it suddenly occurred to him that she was staying for six weeks. What about the wedding? What had happened?

He had a million questions, but he was distracted by Ian, who shuffled up beside him. "Hey, it's Britt."

"Hi, Ian," she said softly, without looking at him. She stood where she was, as though frozen in place, presumably staring back at Rory behind those dark sunglasses.

"I'll get her bags, Mrs. T," said Ian, who took Brittany's suitcases from the back of the golf cart and carried them into Lady Margaret. When he came back out, he joined Mrs. Toffle in the cart. "Drive me back up for lunch?"

"Of course, dear," said Mrs. Toffle to Ian. Then she

turned to Brittany. "Welcome back to Summerhaven, Miss Manion. I hope…well, I hope it's just what you need, dear."

"Thank you," said Brittany, her voice breaking on the word *you*.

As Mrs. Toffle backed up the golf cart and started back up the hill toward the dining room and office, Brittany removed her glasses, pushing them up on her head.

Rory heard his sharp intake of breath—her eyes were puffy and bloodshot, as if she'd been crying for days. "What—what's wrong, Britt? What happened?"

A sob tore from her throat as she stepped forward, and Rory's arms opened just in time as she fell against him. "He—he w-went back to h-his ex."

Wrapping her up against him, the shoulder of his T-shirt absorbing her tears, he felt his heart lurch with a combination of feelings: fury that Dr. Douche would hurt a woman as sweet as Brittany, and sadness for her, that her dreams of getting married and starting a family had been crushed. He hurt for her—really hurt, from his head to his toes and everywhere in between—but he sure wouldn't mind being alone in a dark alley with her ex-fiancé for a few minutes. He knew which one of them would walk away alive.

"I'm sorry, *mo mhuirnín*," he whispered near her ear, holding her tighter as she sobbed against him. "I'm so sorry this happened to you. You deserve so much better."

"He was s-smart and t-talented and a g-g-great dad," she stuttered, her broken voice making Rory feel helpless. "But he d-didn't w-want me."

"His *fucking* loss, Britt. *His* loss. Not yours," he growled.

"I was so c-close," she grieved, "to having everything I always w-wanted."

"And what's that, sweetheart?" he murmured.

"A h-husband and k-kids. A f-family to love." She sniffled, and it was a ragged sound that made his heart twist in his chest.

"You'll still have that," said Rory, leaning back a little to look into her watery eyes. "I promise you. You'll have all that one day. Just not with him."

She took a deep breath, reaching up to wipe her cheeks. Realizing for the first time how intimately he was holding her, two bright spots of red appeared in her cheeks and she stepped back. Though he would have happily held her forever, Rory loosened his arms and let her go.

"I'm just f-feeling sorry for myself," she said with another ragged sniffle. She looked up at him, offering him a sad, small smile, and it took every ounce of strength for him not to reach for her again. "I'm…a mess. I j-just…I feel so raw, Rory. I wanted to come here and…I don't know—heal a little, I guess. I thought you could keep my deposit and I'd come and stay for a few weeks. Sort out my head a little…get away from Boston. Just have some quiet time to heal."

Rory nodded, putting his hands on his hips. "Of course. I'm glad you thought of me—I mean, of us. Of Summerhaven."

"I *did* think of you." She wiped her eyes and smiled again, a little broader this time. "Though I didn't imagine myself crying all over you the second I arrived."

"Eh," he said, brushing at the wet spot on his T-shirt. "Consider it part of the service."

"You're kind," she said, taking a deep breath and looking at Lady Margaret. "I'm so glad she was free."

"Are you sure you want six weeks?" asked Rory. "You don't have to get back? For work?"

"I took a leave of absence from my foundation so I could plan my…" She sniffled again, letting her voice trail off.

"Stay as long as you need," he said, eager to head off her thoughts. "Our first summer week doesn't start until June 4. It's yours until then."

"Thank you," she said. "It's exactly where I want to be."

He watched as she turned and stepped over to the cottage, opening the screen door.

"Britt," he said, wanting to do more for her, hating to leave her alone, even though that's probably what she needed, "do you want to have dinner with me and Ian tonight?"

"I don't think I'd be very good company," she said softly.

"That doesn't matter to us. We—"

"Another time," she said, stepping into the cabin and closing the door behind her.

Rory stood rooted on the spot, half hoping she'd come running back out again and he could hold her for a while longer. But there was no sound at all from her cabin, and after a few minutes, Rory backed away, walking numbly back over to Trinity and climbing up the ladder.

He grabbed his cup of Dunkin' Donuts iced coffee and sucked on the straw, then sat back, knees bent, staring out at the lake. He actively hated Dr. Douche's guts, and his heart ached for Britt, but underneath his anger and sympathy, a different feeling came quietly rumbling to life. Although he couldn't name it, he immediately recognized parts of it: hope and excitement, wild attraction and intense longing. And suddenly, it was though an invisible cord he'd never noticed bound his beating heart to the one beating three cabins away.

A male loon defending his territory somewhere on the lake issued a tremolo, and Rory looked toward the sound but saw nothing except water and woods.

She's injured, his conscience whispered.

But she won't always be, his heart replied.

He took another sip of watered-down coffee, then set the cup aside, crawling up the little roof to the place where he'd been working. Shoving a roof shingle into place, he nailed it into the frame.

Put up your dukes or move along; love is the biggest battle there is.

June's advice echoed in Rory's head, and though he'd never been in love, nor given it much thought until lately, Rory wondered what he wouldn't do to win…if the prize was Brittany Manion's heart.

chapter ten

After leaving Ben at the hospital on Tuesday, Brittany had raced home, falling on her bed for a long cry. She'd briefly considered reaching out to Ben and demanding to see him; had she been too hasty in giving the ring back? Should she have forgiven him and tried to figure out a way to make things work between them? But then she reminded herself that Ben was still in love with his ex-wife and wanted to rebuild his life with her. There was no place for Brittany in that equation anymore. It was just hard to get her head around the fact that yesterday, she'd been an engaged woman in a tiff with her fiancé…and today, suddenly, she was utterly and completely single all over again.

On Wednesday, she'd packed up Ben's things—a toiletry bag, some slippers, and a few changes of clothes he'd left at her place—in a box and had her doorman arrange for them to be delivered to his apartment. And then she'd ordered garlic bread, fettucine alfredo, tortellini in pesto sauce, and tiramisu from Toscana, gorging herself until her stomach hurt.

On Thursday, she'd contacted her parents and close friends via e-mail, telling them, in as few words as possible, that she and Ben had decided to call things off. Her father offered a curt reply about last-minute schedule changes being irritating to his wife, and her mother offered a breezy condolence, asking if Brittany wanted to visit her in Tuscany to "get over things." Hallie had offered to come over with two pints of Ben & Jerry's ice cream, and Brittany had briefly considered it but decided against it. Her friend had enough on her plate with her divorce and custody proceedings; she didn't need the added burden of nursing Brittany's broken heart.

On Friday morning, she'd stopped by A Better Tomorrow, but the staff she'd left in charge of her foundation had everything in hand, and besides, with her red-rimmed eyes and forlorn face, she wasn't exactly inspiring to the recovering addicts they were trying to build up. She'd headed back to her apartment, which felt vast and empty without the promise of little feet pitter-pattering down the hall in a year or two.

In fact, her home was suddenly unbearable, and the thought of joining her mother and Gilles—who liked to sunbathe nude and make love wherever and whenever the mood hit them—in Tuscany made her cringe. Though she did like the idea of getting away. She wanted an escape from her friends and her apartment, from Boston and everything else that reminded her of Ben. And only one place felt right—felt like the perfect place to heal: Summerhaven. Without making a reservation, she'd packed four large suitcases, wheeled them down to the parking garage, shoved them in her car, and set out for New Hampshire.

By noon, she was there.

By a quarter past twelve, she was crying on Rory Haven's shoulder.

And by one o'clock, she was fast asleep between crisp

white sheets, a thick down comforter the only armor she needed against the outside world.

She slept for twenty hours, waking up at nine o'clock the next morning, already feeling a bit better. Distance from her real life, it seemed, relieved the tightness in her chest and the throbbing of her head. And when she got dressed and took a walk down to the lake, breathing the clean New Hampshire air deeply, her tears were scattered and few. She sat on a dock by the water for hours, thinking about her broken engagement, and found that losing Ben hurt far less than she'd expected it to.

She and Ben had fallen fast and furious for each other—they'd only dated for nine months before becoming engaged—but they'd never lived together and never gone on vacation together. Ben had never really invited her into his life with his daughters, whom she'd only met a couple of times, and she'd only introduced Ben to her parents once, at her mother's annual Christmas party in Boston. They didn't have a lot in common—Ben loved exercise and healthy eating, and his phone was practically attached to his wrist, whereas Brittany preferred to relax on the beach with a book and could take or leave her phone most days, unless she was expecting an important call. Even their musical taste was different, Ben preferring the music that had been popular during his college years, when Brittany was only a toddler.

Were you in love with him? Or just in love with the idea *of him?*

If she was truly in love with Ben, she knew that her pain should be unbearable now. But it wasn't; it was bearable. In fact, if she was being honest, there were even moments when she felt more than a twinge of relief, as if part of her had known all along that Ben wouldn't have been able to make her happy in the long run.

As the hours on the Summerhaven dock drifted by, Brittany had to admit that what she'd really fallen in love with was a vision of her future that included her adoring pediatrician husband and their two or three lovely children. But while she was daydreaming, she'd lost sight of reality, which included a reluctant, apparently philandering fiancé who was still in love with his ex-wife and had kept his vasectomy a secret from her.

It only took two days for Brittany to firmly believe what she'd started to recognize the moment she returned her engagement ring to Ben: she had dodged a bullet in losing him.

Unfortunately, however, that knowledge didn't totally assuage her pain. Tears still brimmed in her eyes. She was still hurting deeply. And that's when she realized that her lasting sorrow didn't stem from Ben's loss; it was born of a different and more visceral, terrifying place. It was the paralyzing fear of remaining unloved forever.

Brittany was already insecure after her breakup with Travis, especially after learning of his quick remarriage. Coupled with Ben's rejection, her self-confidence and self-worth hit an all-time low. Sitting by the lake on her own all weekend, she wondered over and over again:

What's wrong with me?

Am I unlovable?

Because that's sure how it feels.

As she walked back to Lady Margaret from the lake on Sunday evening, she saw Rory's truck approaching from the main path and paused to say hello when he rolled down the window.

"Hey, Britt."

"Hi, Rory."

His beautiful green eyes were troubled but gentle. "I don't want to bother you, so no pressure…but I'm headed over to Tierney's for dinner. Just wondering if you'd like to come along."

"Oh," she said, mustering a small smile. "Thank her for me, but I think I'll stay here."

He cocked his head to the side, flicking a glance to Lady Margaret. "There's no kitchen in there, and I haven't seen your car leave campus once. What're you surviving on?"

"I brought some energy bars from home."

Rory pursed his lips and gave her a look. "You can't live on energy bars. Come on, Britt. Join us. Tierney's making a roast and mashed potatoes."

Mashed potatoes. *Swoon.* How long had it been since Brittany had dug into a plate of mashed potatoes? Besides, maybe she could use the company of the rowdy but loving Haven siblings.

"Are you sure? I bet I'll be crap company."

"Ah, Brittany," he said with an Irish accent that sounded like his mother and made her grin, "our expectations are not pure high. We won't give out either way. I promise."

She wasn't totally certain what he'd just said, but she had to crack a smile at his persistence. "Okay, fine. I'll come."

"Grand!"

"Just let me get changed," she said, looking down and wrinkling her nose at her jeans and T-shirt.

"No need," said Rory, hopping from the cab of his

truck. "You look fine."

"Are you sure?" she asked.

His eyes started at her feet and slowly tracked up her body, making her feel warm all over. "Positive."

Before she could protest again, he pivoted, rounded the front of the truck, and opened her door.

"I have nothing to bring Tierney," she said, following him and climbing into the passenger side of his truck. "I hate to go empty-handed."

"Tierney won't expect a thing."

"It doesn't feel right. My mother would throw a fit if she knew I arrived at a dinner party without a hostess gift."

"Dinner party," scoffed Rory. "You've got it all wrong. This is just a Sunday supper, not a dinner party. Just a casual family thing."

A family thing. Something inside of her squeezed in a way that was painful for a moment and then suddenly lovely, because it *was* a family thing, wasn't it? But for once, she wasn't on the outside looking in; she was invited, she was included, she was welcome.

"Would you feel better if we stopped at a florist?" asked Rory, backing out of Oxford Row and heading up the main path.

"I would," said Brittany. "Oh, but wait! My purse! It's back at Lady Margaret!"

Rory chuckled softly. "I'll make you a loan. I'm fairly certain you're good for it."

Buckling her seat belt, she nodded. "Okay." She wasn't dressed for dinner, didn't have her purse, and had no gift for Tierney. "I'm a mess."

"You're too hard on yourself." After a few minutes of

bouncing along in silence, Rory glanced at her. "Are you doing okay? I've been worried about you, but I didn't want to intrude."

"Thanks for that," she said. "The alone time's been good for me, actually. I've been sorting things out. Getting clarity. And I mean, at least I'm not crying all over you anymore, right?"

"Never said I minded you crying on me, Britt."

"Why are you so sweet?" she asked, blinking away unexpected tears as she looked over at him, her glance resting on his strong, smooth jaw and tracing the lines of his beautiful profile. Her cheeks were still warm from the way he'd just looked at her, but she squelched the tiny thrum of hope from deep, deep within her heart.

Don't be ridiculous, Brittany. He's just being kind to you for old time's sake, or because you're a guest at his camp. Don't read into it.

You're nothing special—you should know that by now.

He shrugged. "I'm nothing special."

She would have gasped at the parallel between her thoughts and his words if her whole being hadn't clenched in protest.

Rory Haven was special. Always had been. Always would be.

"Yes, you are," she said softly, swiping at her tired eyes as she turned to look out the windshield. "*Believe me*, you are."

As it turned out, coaxing Britt to a family dinner with his siblings was the first step in forcing her out of hiding.

The next morning, Mrs. Toffle stopped by Brittany's

cabin with a paperback copy of Leylah Attar's *Mists of the Serengeti*. She said she hoped that Britt was a fast reader because they'd be discussing it at book group on Thursday night. For the next four days, Rory didn't see Britt unless she was lugging that beautiful book around the campground.

From what he heard from Mrs. Toffle on Friday morning, she not only held her own at book club but reduced the other ladies to weeping with her tenderhearted analysis of the main characters.

More than once he found Brittany standing beneath one of the cottages that Ian was reshingling, gleefully trading insults with his brother like it was her job.

"...yeah, well, if I see any fancy, hotshot, Boston doctors lingering around, I'll send them your way."

"Oh, you're so sweet! And if I find a fifth of vodka lying around, I'll make sure to tell you where you can find it."

"Fantastic. Hey, Manion, do you know what shithead doctors and pretentious hotels have in common?"

"No. Tell me."

"You."

"What do *you* know? There's too much blood in your alcohol system."

On and on it went—razor-sharp jibes and clever retorts that ended with Brittany giggling and Ian chortling with glee.

Though Ian's attention to Britt bugged Rory on one level, he couldn't help enjoying their repartee. He liked it that Britt wasn't all sugared peaches and thick cream. She was capable of a little friendly sparring when the mood struck her, and as long as their back-and-forth never crossed a line from sibling-like tussling to something more, Rory enjoyed overhearing it. And he appreciated the way her chipper presence seemed to help Ian brood less.

Two weeks after she'd arrived at Summerhaven, Rory noticed that she'd appear at the north dining room every day at one and leave again a little before two. When he discovered that Chef Jamie was testing new recipes on Brittany, Mrs. Toffle, and his wife, Cheryl, who'd also been coerced into Thursday Night Book Group, Rory made sure to linger near the dining hall around two every day.

Meeting up with her on the path, he'd walk her back to her cottage, learning little things about her life: where she went to college (Dickinson), the part of Boston she loved best (Cambridge), the name of her first dog (Rodolfo, a grouchy Pekinese), and her favorite ski resort (Smuggler's Notch in Vermont, which surprised him, since he'd been expecting something tonier, like Aspen or Chamonix). She liked chilled Rieslings from Austria and the occasional Tito's martini (dirty, with olives). She didn't mind cold winters but hated hot summers, preferred lakes to the ocean, and chose paperback books over an e-reader because she liked the tactile sensation of paper beneath her fingers.

After her third Sunday dinner at Tierney's, Rory strolled over to her cabin on Monday morning with an old, but working, coffeemaker for her room. Not that she'd asked for it, but her gratitude had sure made the gesture worthwhile.

"Thank you!" she gushed. "I love it."

"It's not a Keurig or anything."

"Yes, but now I can have *hot* coffee," she said, gesturing to the small army of Starbucks single-serving bottles on her windowsill that she'd been purchasing from the local gas station.

"And I have something else for you," he said, hoping that he wasn't being too forward with his next gesture.

He knew that she ate breakfast in her cabin, lunch in the dining room with the ladies, dinner with him and his siblings on Wednesdays and Sundays and with the book group on Thursdays, but he wanted her to have a place where she could make herself a meal anytime she wanted.

Pulling a key to his apartment out of his pocket, he offered it to her. "I want you to use my kitchen anytime you want. You can keep groceries in the fridge and use the stove or microwave. Just come and go as you please, okay?"

She stared at him, frozen, then glanced down at the key.

Shit. Was this too much? He wasn't trying to make a move on her...was he? Fuck, his motivations were getting cloudier by the day.

"Um. You don't have to..."

He started to pull his hand back, but she reached out and covered his hand with hers, gently wrestling open his fingers to reveal the key.

"You're awfully good to me, Rory." His breathing hitched from the tenderness in her big brown eyes, from the way her hand cradled his. She took the key and smiled at him as she slipped it into her pocket. "Thank you."

"It's nothing," he said.

"It's something to me," she said softly, her tongue darting out to wet her lips.

"I should have thought of it sooner." He felt his cheeks flushing and took a deep breath, turning away from her. This woman. Damn, but this woman was so far under his skin by now. "So, uh, come by anytime."

The following evening, she'd knocked at his door.

146

"I hope you don't mind," she said when he answered.

"Why didn't you use your key?" he asked, taking the two bags of groceries from her arms and walking them into the kitchen.

She shrugged, smiling sheepishly. "Felt funny."

"You shouldn't," he said. "You should have somewhere to fix yourself something when you're hungry."

That evening, she'd tried making her first frozen meal in the oven but hadn't removed the food from the plastic container or pulled away the cellophane covering. They were watching an episode of *This Is Us* when s terrible smell started wafting into the living room from the kitchen, followed by a billow of gray smoke. When Rory had opened the oven, he'd found her dinner in a melted heap of macaroni, cheese, and plastic.

After he made her a quick omelet and buttered toast so she wouldn't go hungry, she'd fallen asleep on the couch beside him with her head on his shoulder, the scent of her vanilla shampoo making it impossible to concentrate on anything except for the sweet woman beside him.

For someone so wealthy, she was surprisingly tender and vulnerable. All Rory wanted to do was wrap her up in his arms, safe and secure, and never let her go. The longing in his heart had become a living, breathing thing that grew day by day until he didn't live his life by a calendar and watch—he lived it by Brittany.

At eight, Britt takes her coffee to the dock…

At ten, Britt takes a jog…

At one, Britt slips into the dining hall…

At two, Britt and I take a walk…

At five on Wednesdays and Sundays, I pick her up for

dinner…

At six on Thursdays, she goes to book club…

And on and on.

Little by little, she laughed more and sighed less, her lips tilted up in a warm smile for everyone in the small community of Summerhaven employees. In fact, at some point over the three weeks she'd been staying in Lady Margaret, she'd somehow become the heart of the camp.

And yet, when she didn't think anyone was watching, he noted that melancholy was never far behind her sweet smiles and musical giggles. Infinitely less broken than she'd been on the day she arrived, she still seemed cautious, as evidenced by the way she'd shied away from accepting Rory's first invitation to dinner at Tierney's or the way she'd scanned his face before accepting the key to his place. Like a puppy who's been hit one too many times and flinches from a well-meaning hand, he could see that Brittany didn't quite trust the people around her, though he sensed that she desperately wanted to.

As far as he could tell, she hadn't talked to Dr. Douche since arriving at Summerhaven three weeks ago, but he was certain that the gentle but omnipresent melancholy that surrounded her had a great deal to do with the loss of the fiancé she probably still loved.

Sometimes it annoyed Rory that she missed him. Why should she feel sad about someone who didn't deserve her? About this asshole who'd hurt her?

She sighed in her sleep, snuggling closer to Rory on the couch, and his body, already on fire for her, tightened, his blood sluicing to his groin and pooling there like liquid heat. He had feelings for Britt, but he was also wildly attracted to her. Glancing down at his crotch, the uncomfortable evidence of his arousal bulged against his jeans and he grunted softly, easing himself away from her.

Gently lowering her head to the couch, he slipped a pillow under her blonde waves and covered her body with a blanket. Then he turned off the TV and the lights, taking a long look at his beautiful Brittany before whispering, "*Oíche mhaith, mo mhuirnín.*"

"Night, Rory," she whispered back in her sleep. "Thank you."

chapter eleven

Even though he'd insisted about a hundred times that she should just use her key and walk in the door of his apartment, Brittany still felt like she should knock on the door when she knew Rory was home. As days turned into weeks, she'd compromised by cracking the door and calling, "Rory? It's me" every time she stopped by, which was almost every night.

"In here," he called from the kitchen.

"Sorry to bother you," she said, hanging her jacket on a peg by the front door and toeing off her shoes before walking through the living room toward the sound of his voice.

"You're not a bother, Britt. You know that."

She peeked around the doorway into the kitchen. "I was hoping to make myself a grilled cheese for dinner."

He looked up from where he sat at the kitchen table with a cup of coffee, surrounded by paperwork, and so handsome, he took her breath away. His eyes sparkled when he grinned at her.

"Are you going to take the cellophane off the cheese slices first?"

"That was over a week ago!" she protested. "You're never going to let me live that down, are you?"

"Probably not," he said, smiling at her over the rim of his coffee mug as he took a sip. "Is this one of Jamie's recipes?"

"Nope. Cheryl. But I promise you, it's so good, you won't believe it. You want one?" She put her hands on her hips, giving him what she hoped was a sharp look. "If you say no, you're missing out, boyo."

"*Boyo*? Now where'd you pick that up from?"

She chuckled, squatting down to open the cabinet that held the frying pans. "Ian, probably."

"Bad bloody influence," muttered Rory.

Brittany looked up in time to see him checking out her ass and gave him a sassy look as she stood up. "See anything you like?"

"Plenty," he said, his eyes darkening just a touch.

"Cheeky," she replied, turning around to face the stove so he wouldn't see the bloom of pleasure in her cheeks.

She lit the burner as Rory had taught her and let the pan heat up as she turned to the refrigerator and withdrew a loaf of multigrain bread and deli-sliced packages of cheddar and gruyere cheese she'd purchased from the gourmet market in Holderness.

"So?" she prompted, leaning over the table to grab the butter that sat in a dish near his papers. "You want?"

"I want," said Rory, his voice low, his breathing deep and audible as she picked up the butter, straightened, and stepped back from the table.

A dozen of butterflies took flight in her stomach at the look on his face.

"Rory?" she murmured, wondering if you could drown in someone else's eyes.

He stared at her for a beat before looking away and answering with a gravelly voice, "Yes, I want a sandwich."

She turned back to the stove, her heart galloping as she put the sandwiches together and placed the first one in the frying pan. "You're working hard."

His voice was back to normal when he answered. "Mm-hm. The Carrolls. Mr. and Mrs. Franklin Carroll are celebrating their sixtieth anniversary here this weekend…with fifty of their closest friends and family members."

"Sixty years." Brittany sighed as she flipped over the sandwich as Cheryl had taught her. "That's so romantic. Anything I can help with?"

"Well…let's see…I've got Mrs. T in the office doing check-in, Doug on top of housekeeping, Ian handling the luggage…"

"And who is offering warmth and hospitality?" asked Brittany, sliding the first sandwich onto a plate and placing the second in the sizzling-hot pan.

"You?" he guessed with a smile in his voice.

That was one of the things she liked most about Rory—the way that his voice conveyed so much emotion. One minute, it was low and serious—furious that Ben had hurt her or worried about Ian's sobriety. Another minute, it was tinged with humor, gently laughing at her for not knowing how to make a frozen dinner or pointing out that if she didn't wander through poison ivy, she wouldn't have a rash around her ankles. And other moments, like now, it was filled with warmth. If a voice could smile, Rory Haven's knew how, and it just about made her breathless to hear it.

"Yes. Me," she confirmed. "And how about bouquets

of wildflowers in every room? I can arrange them. I'm good at that."

"I believe it. You're amazing at everything."

"Arranging wildflowers doesn't make me amazing," she said, smiling to herself as she flipped over his sandwich.

"If it adds something to the guest experience, but not to my workload, it definitely makes you amazing."

Though she'd denied the compliment, inside, her heart swelled from his words.

When she'd arrived at Summerhaven four weeks ago, she'd been a shell of herself. Rejected, abandoned, and betrayed by the two men who were supposed to spend their lives loving her, she truly questioned whether she would ever find happiness. And perhaps most terrifying of all, with the loss of her fiancé, she hadn't been able to visualize the future she wanted anymore. Instead of seeing a beautiful house in the Boston suburbs with Ben and their children, she saw...nothing.

Loneliness.

Sorrow.

Unending longing.

But then she'd arrived at Summerhaven and fallen into Rory Haven's waiting arms. Strengthened by the blessing of new and unexpected friendships, day by day she'd grieved less and healed more. In fact, surrounded by Mrs. Toffle, Doug, Jamie, Cheryl, and the marvelous Havens, she found she wasn't lonely at all anymore.

But strangest of all was the dawning realization that she was—*right here, right now*—the happiest she'd ever been in all her adult life. And while she treasured all the personalities that made up the fabric of Summerhaven, none so affected her heart as Rory. It didn't hurt that he was achingly beautiful, with his dark hair and flashing green eyes, but it was so much more than his rugged good looks. He made her feel like she wasn't worthless, like she had something to offer, like she was wanted and even needed. He made her feel like she *belonged* somewhere, which was the greatest balm of all to her healing heart.

And no, she didn't know what her future looked like anymore, nor did she try to visualize it or force it into being by the sheer power of her longing for it. Every day held a new surprise or discovery—like the fact that two different kind of cheeses made a grilled cheese sandwich taste better or the fact that Rory was more cheerful on rainy days—and instead of living for the promise of tomorrow, she lived for the miracles of today…little blessings everywhere.

She slid the second sandwich onto a plate and turned off the burner, bringing both sandwiches to the table and sitting down across from Rory.

"*Bon appétit.*"

She watched his face as he lifted the grilled cheese to his mouth and took a bite, taking immense pleasure in the way his eyes fluttered closed in bliss. "Mmm. Britt. Oh, man, that's good!"

Beaming with pride, she chuckled softly. "I *told* you."

He took another wolfish bite. "You are welcome to come and make me a grilled cheese anytime, woman."

Woman.

It was such a raw and sexy thing to call her. Primitive. Elemental.

Her pride had taken a terrible blow when she discovered that Ben had slept with Angie while they were still engaged. Comparing herself to dark, petite Angie had made her feel clumsy and unsexy; she blamed her curves (and love of pasta) for Ben's wandering eye and wondered if she was woman enough to hold on to a man.

But Rory had a way of talking, a way of looking at her, that made her feel like the most desirable woman on creation. And though she knew her heart probably couldn't bear a third rejection so soon, his attraction to her, coupled with his kindness, touched her deeply. She felt herself falling toward him, into him, for him. She couldn't help it. Every time they were together, the air hissed and crackled between them like it was charged by a live wire, and it was getting harder to ignore it…especially because she liked it so damn much.

She didn't believe that Rory was dating anyone, though she wasn't with him all the time, of course. It was completely possible that he had a casual relationship with someone she just didn't know about. Ignoring the way that thought fell like a rock to the pit of her stomach, she looked up from her sandwich.

"So…wildflowers and warm smiles. Anything else?"

He grabbed a napkin from the basket in the center of the table and swiped at his mouth. "Well…Doug's off tomorrow night, and I was going to ask Ian to help me rope lights in the barn. I promised white twinkle lights for the dance they're having on Saturday night. But if *you* wanted to help me—"

"Yes! I'm your girl!"

He'd been raising the last bite of sandwich to his lips, but he froze, staring at her with wide eyes. Finally he blinked, popping the rest of the sandwich into his mouth and chewing slowly.

Your girl? Geez, Brittany. Way to be subtle.

"I mean…I'm not your girl. That's ridiculous. I just—I'm happy to help."

"Huh," he muttered, standing up to take his plate to the sink. "Sure you wouldn't mind?"

"Nope. It's a date!"

A date? A date, Brittany? She cringed. *Desperate much?*

He paused at the sink with his back to her, but unless her eyes deceived her, she saw the muscles of his back ripple and his shoulders snap back. He turned around, his eyes wide and searching. "Um, a *date*?"

"No!" she exclaimed. "No. Oh my God. No. Not a date. I wasn't trying to…I didn't mean we were—I only *meant*, tomorrow is the *date* that we will rope lights together in the barn."

He raised his eyebrows with an inscrutable look. "Okay. So…you're not my girl, and tomorrow's not a date."

"Exactly," she reconfirmed, hating—with every beat of her heart—that she wasn't his girl and that tomorrow wasn't a date.

But after all, she reminded herself, just because her heart had seized on him lately in a reprisal of her teenage crush didn't mean (1) that she was ready to date anyone and, much more important, (2) that he was at all interested in dating her anyway.

"Okay. How about I pick up my not-girl for our not-date at five tomorrow? I'll drive us over to the barn."

"Sure," she said weakly, wishing she could just erase the last two minutes of her life. "That's fine."

Last night had been interesting, to say the least. The double whammy combination of "I'm your girl" and "It's a date" had actually made Rory's body *shudder* with longing. But then, he thought acidly, all was right again in his world when she clarified that she'd misspoken. Because why would beautiful, rich, incredibly amazing Brittany Manion be interested in small-time camp owner Rory Haven?

As he'd reminded himself a thousand times over the past month, she was a temporary fixture at Summerhaven. She was only here to get over her broken engagement, and once she was strong enough to return to *her* world, she'd leave.

He just wished that this realization was enough to keep him from falling for her, but sadly, it was not. And the day she left, he'd face a long road of mending the remains of his own tattered heart.

It didn't matter. Even knowing that he'd feel her loss everywhere once she left, it didn't stop him from spending all the time with her that he could. It didn't even stop him—rule-follower and realist that he generally was—from making the most of that time and hoping, in the deepest reaches of his heart where fantasies lived, that she *wouldn't* leave. That somehow, someway, she'd stay with him. Forever.

It was a delicate situation. On one hand, he still considered her an injured woman and wouldn't dream of "making a move" on her. But on the other, the idea of letting her go without a fight made his self-loathing rise like the tide during a full moon. So he lived in limbo, quietly yearning and falling a little harder for her every day.

He looked over at her, dressed in dark jeans and a white button-down shirt, standing on a ladder and using thumbtacks to secure a rope of white lights around a ceiling rafter. As she raised her arms to wind the string again, her shirt untucked from the waistband of her pants and rode up a little to reveal a strip of soft white skin. His heart raced and his fingers twitched, but he looked away quickly—she was catching him staring more and more lately, and he didn't want to make her uncomfortable.

"How was book club on Thursday?" he asked, trying to get a safe conversation going.

"Great. We talked about Leylah Attar's *The Paper Swan*."

"Good book?"

"Phenomenal," she said. "It was so raw and passionate, and…" She sighed. "Yeah. It was something, all right."

"Mrs. T loves it that you joined her group," he said. "You fit in really well here, Britt."

As soon as the words left his mouth, he grimaced. *Talk about desperate!*

"I love being here," she said. "Truly. I'm so grateful. I was—well, I was mess when I arrived, wasn't I?"

He didn't answer, just opened another accordion-style paper lantern, thinking, *Yeah, you were, because you'd been hurt by your asshole fiancé.* And then suddenly, without warning, without thinking, he heard himself asking her, "So…have you heard from Dr. Douche since you've been here?"

"Dr.—" She chortled, turning to look at him with wide eyes. "Oh, my God. You're as terrible as Ian when you want to be! 'Dr. Douche.'" She hooted with laughter before sobering up. "That's not very nice, Rory."

"Does he deserve *nice*?"

What was left of her smile faded quickly. "Not even a little bit."

"You never told me what happened."

"I never told you the sad tale of my pathetic love life?" She took a deep breath. "Hand me another rope." He crossed to the table and picked up another strand of white lights, handing it to her while she gazed down at him. "Well, in a nutshell, my husband and I divorced because he didn't want kids. But not long after, I found a picture of him on Facebook, married with a baby. That same night, I met Ben, and I thought it was fate. A pediatrician with two kids of his own? Oh, yeah. This guy was 100 percent, bona fide father material. Or so I thought." She paused before continuing. "But I found out two things on the morning we broke up: one, that he'd had a vasectomy…and two, that he'd cheated on me with his ex-wife."

"Britt," he gasped, feeling her words like a sucker punch to the jaw. "Shit."

"Yeah. Turns out he didn't want any more kids…nor did he want to be with me."

"What an *asshole*," Rory growled, feeling pure hatred bubbling up from his gut like lava.

"You got it."

"Motherfucker."

"Exactly. The mother of his girls, to be specific."

It took him a second, but as soon as he got her dark joke, he laughed, though his amusement was short-lived. "Damn, Britt. I am so sorry."

"For what?" She shrugged, uncoiling the lights, her voice lighter when she spoke again. "Did he hurt me? Yes.

But even I'm smart enough to see that we weren't meant to be."

"Sure…but at what cost?" He thought about that look on her face sometimes—the one that reminded him of an abused puppy. "You know that none of that is your fault, right?"

He grabbed the side of the ladder she was standing on, gazing up at her. She held the lights limply in her hands as her eyes brightened with tears, and he felt compelled to say more, to do more, to try to help her see herself the way he saw her.

"He was a damned fool to let you go, Britt."

She gulped softly, nodding at him before mustering a brave smile. "That's kind. Thanks, Rory."

"Don't do that," he said sharply. "They're not just words. I *mean* them."

She sniffled, smiling a little wider. "Well, I meant what I said too. I dodged a bullet with Ben. Honestly, whatever hurt I feel is more because of his rejection than losing him. That's the truth."

It blew Rory's mind that any man who had a chance with her could dream of risking her. That two such men still roamed the earth made Rory fear for the stupidity of his gender.

"It wasn't about you, Britt."

"I just got two duds, huh?" She looked skeptical. "You're sweet, but since they have me in common, odds are that it *is* about me…at least, in part."

Rory vehemently disagreed.

He was convinced that she'd just had bad luck, and that yes, her two choices had been "duds," as she said. But the look on her face told him he wasn't going to be able to convince her of it right here, right now, so he didn't try.

Eager to change the subject and lighten the mood, however, he asked her, "Hey, do you mind if I put on some music? I made a playlist of hits from 1957 for the dance on Saturday."

"Go for it," she said. "Hey, are there more thumbtacks somewhere?"

He walked over to the folding table in the center of the barn and grabbed a handful for her, then took his iPhone out of his pocket and chose the playlist for the Carrolls' Saturday evening dance, synching it to the barn's Bluetooth speakers.

The Diamonds' "Little Darlin'" started playing, the sounds of castanets and a cow bell instantly filling the room. Rory took a deep breath and smiled, remembering his parents dancing to 1950s music in their kitchen when he and his siblings were little.

"My parents loved fifties music," said Rory. "They weren't even born until the midsixties, but I guess my grandmother had it on all the time."

"Your mother's mother?"

"Yeah," he said. "Patsy Kelley. She was from Killarney."

"Your mom's accent was strong," said Brittany. "I remember it."

"Still is," said Rory, thinking of the last time he'd visit his parents over a weekend in March. "Her speech is improving."

"I'm so sorry about her stroke."

Rory climbed back up his own ladder and nailed a paper

lantern over the strand of lights that Brittany had left hanging in her progress.

"Yeah, it sucks," he said, a shiver rocking him as he remembered his race to the hospital at Dartmouth. "How're your parents?"

"Fine. My mother lives in France with her boyfriend, and my dad is remarried in Seattle."

"You don't see them much?"

"I spent Christmas with my father and his wife, and I go visit my mother a couple of times a year…" Her voice drifted off, the unspoken words louder than the ones she'd shared: she was pretty alone in the world when it came to family. "Can I ask you a totally random question?"

"Anything," he said as the Del Vikings' started singing "Come Go with Me."

"How come you…?" She took a deep breath and let it go quickly. "I mean—no. Forget it."

Rory climbed down the ladder and grabbed another lantern. "After that windup? Nope. Unacceptable. Now you *have* to ask."

She glanced at him, offering a shy smile. "Okay. I was just wondering…how come you never talked to me? I mean, when I was a camper here. Ian was friendly—maybe a little *too* friendly," she amended with a small chuckle, "but you and Tierney acted like we were all invisible."

Oh, man. If she only knew how he'd lusted after her, watching her, wondering about her, wishing he had the courage to defy his parents, break their rules, and make a move on her.

"My mother's ultimate rule: 'No fraternizin' with the guests.'"

"Why?"

"Well, for two reasons. The first was that if one of us dated a guest and things went sideways, she and my dad could lose business. The second reason, which I think was much more important to her, was that she was always aware of her place. I know that sounds weird in America, but Ireland's a lot more class conscious, and she wasn't from a wealthy family. My grandmother was the cook at a"—he adopted a strong brogue, rolling his *r* like his mother—"gr-r-r-eat house. My mother was taught not ter mix wi' her betters, an' that's what she taught us too."

"Her...*betters*?"

He nodded. "People wealthier, more educated, of a higher social class..."

"God, you must have hated us," muttered Brittany, her expression bordering on horrified, "having to drive us around and plan our activities, but not even able to have a conversation."

"Nah," said Rory. "I hated the rule, not the people. And certainly not you."

She gave him a small smile. "What happened if you broke her rules?"

"You remember my mother, right?" Rory laughed as he nailed another lantern into place. "She's an Irish mother. She'd die for us, sure, but when we were bad? Well, she wasn't afraid to use the spoon."

"The *spoon*?" asked Brittany with wide eyes.

"A wooden kitchen spoon...on our arses. An Irish mother's favorite threat."

"Did she ever *actually*—?"

"Are selkies sea-lovin'? Of course! I'd offer to show

you the scars, but I'd have to drop my pants."

"Scars?" gasped Brittany, flicking a look at his ass.

"No. Not really. No scars." Rory laughed as he climbed down the ladder to collect another lantern. "Though, the spoon was real. I was on the receiving end more than once. Now, Ian?" He chuckled again. "Jaysus, Mary, an' Joseph, yer man an' that spoon had a *pure* close relationship."

"I can only imagine," she answered, her voice thick with laughter. "He is a terrible rascal."

"But not your type," said Rory quickly, looking up at her on the ladder and feeling like Romeo in the garden looking up at Juliet.

"No, Rory," she said softly, her lips tilting up, her eyes tender. "Ian's not my type at all."

They locked eyes as Sam Cooke's strong voice filled the barn with the gentle, lilting words, *Folks say that you found someone new…*

Rory's mouth dropped open and he smiled up at her. "Oh, my God. *This* song. This is *such* a good song. Come on down here, *mo mhuirnín.*"

She grinned at him, resting the long strand of lights on the top of the ladder and climbing down to stand in front of him.

Without asking her permission, one of his hands landed on her hip, pulling her close, as the other reached for her hand, clasping her fingers in his. "Dance with me?"

Still smiling, her brown eyes filled with something so tender, it made his stomach flip over. She nodded, stepping closer to him as they started moving to the music.

This love of ours could always start anew…

And just like that, Rory was fifteen again, standing in

the shadows of the old barn, watching Brittany Manion dance with one of the Mathison boys. He could still feel it in his gut—that proprietary feeling that made him yearn to smash his fist in Travis Mathison's face and take his place— to feel Brittany Manion's hand clasping his instead, her sweet, soft body pressed against his, her kind brown eyes looking earnestly into his.

Just call my name. I know I'm not ashamed. I'll come running back to you.

Gazing down at her, the past and present intersected seamlessly, his mother's insistence on no fraternizing somehow dovetailing with the eventuality of holding her in his arms one day. He just wished he'd known then. It would have saved him a lot of sleepless nights staring at the ceiling, his adolescent body raging with hormones, hard and desperate, the object of his desire fast asleep down the path in Lady Margaret.

"What are you thinking?" she asked breathlessly.

"What I would have given to do this when I was kid."

Her nerves betrayed her when her face broke into a too-wide smile. "What? No. You never looked my way."

"Sweet girl, I was *always* looking your way."

"Hmm," she hummed, her warm breath gently fanning the base of his throat. "Maybe once or twice, but when I caught you, you'd frown and walk away."

He readjusted his grip on her hand so that their fingers were intertwined. "No fraternizin', remember?"

"But Ian—"

"—broke the rules and got the spoon."

He pulled her closer, crushing her breasts against his chest. He could feel the points of her nipples through her T-shirt, and blood funneled to his groin. Did she want him too? Half as badly as he wanted her?

"Rory," whispered Brittany, her lips so close to his ear that his eyes fluttered closed for a split second, "I wish you'd broken the rules."

His dick hardened as though on command, and he resisted the urge to pull her yet closer, to grind the evidence of his deep desire into the sweet, soft place between her thighs.

"Me too," he managed to grind out.

I've got my pride, but deep down inside, I'm yours and yours alone.

The hand on his shoulder edged its way to the back of his neck, her fingers threading into his hair, her voice soft and deep. "Rory...I've been meaning to ask...what does, um, *mavorneen* mean? You've said it once or twice, and I...I was just..."

Mo mhuirnín.

Drawing back from her just a touch, he looked into her eyes before his gaze slid to her lips. "It's Gaelic for 'my sweetheart.'"

"Oh." She gasped, arching her back just a little bit, her lips parting in welcome as he leaned closer—

"Hey, Rory! Tonight, right? For roping the...oh, shit."

Jolted from the sweetness of the dreamlike moment, Rory's neck whipped left to find Ian standing in the doorway of the barn.

chapter twelve

"*Shite*," muttered Ian, looking back and forth between Brittany and Rory with wide eyes before grimacing. "*Tá brón orm*, Rory."

I'm sorry.

Brittany stiffened in Rory's arms, then stepped away from him, laughing nervously as she darted her glance to Ian and then back to Rory. Her dilated eyes and the bloom in her cheeks made his heart ache as she dropped her hand from the back of his neck and untangled her hand from his.

"I should probably go," she said, her voice low and breathy, her breasts rising and falling with shallow breaths.

Fuck Ian!

"N-No!" stuttered Rory as Sam Cooke wrapped up his song. "It's fine—"

"Stay!" cried Ian. "*I'll* go!"

"Good night, Rory," she said, grabbing her jacket from the table and sticking her tongue out at Ian as she rushed from the barn into the night.

Rory watched her go, knowing that his dick was straining against the front zipper of his jeans for Ian's amusement, but he didn't give a shit. He'd been so close…so close…

"Oh, man…I am so…fucking…sorry," muttered Ian,

still standing by the door.

Rory ran a hand through his hair, considering whether he should run after Britt or let her go. Clenching his jaw and taking a deep breath, he decided to let her go. She didn't need him—and his overeager dick—racing after her into the night.

He blew out a long, frustrated breath. "Well, that sucked. Thanks a ton, Ian."

"I guess we got our wires crossed. I thought…"

"I left a message with Tierney, canceling."

"Huh. Well, I didn't get it. She was still up at the palace when I left." He gestured to the half-finished lights, shrugging out of a tan barn jacket. "Looks like you could use my help finishing up."

"Yeah," muttered Rory. "Fine."

Ian looked up at the lights Rory and Britt had already roped. "So…I was pretty sure, but now I'm positive."

"About…?"

With his usual annoying way of sliding into conversations from the side, Ian rubbed his dark beard and gave his brother a shit-eating grin. "You're in love with her."

"Oh, Christ." She was still healing from her breakup, and Rory wasn't some asshole to push her when she was vulnerable. In fact, it was probably a good thing that Ian interrupted them when he did, all things considered. "She just got dumped."

"Mmm. Not really. That was, like, over a month ago."

"Exactly. It can take a long time to heal from something like that."

"She looks pretty healed to me."

Rory clasped the back of his neck where Brittany's

fingers had just been teasing and gave his brother a look. "Can we not do this right now, man? Can you just help me finish up?"

"She's hot," said Ian, his tone baiting.

Rory dropped his hand and fisted his fingers. "Do *not* go there, Ian. I'm serious."

"Just tell me this," said Ian, placing his hands on his hips and cocking his head to the side, "are you in love with her or not?"

"I barely know her."

"Um, no. That's not true. You've let her get closer to you than anyone else...ever. At this point, I'd say she's edging up on me and Tier. So, answer the question: Do you love her or not?"

"Just shut the fuck up and help me, huh?"

"Sure. I get it." Ian took a deep breath, climbing up the ladder to resume Brittany's work roping the rafters. He looked down at his brother. "Well, you know what, Rory? This is kind of great for me, because she's awesome, and if you're not into her, I think I'll ask her——"

"You do it, and I'll fucking *hurt* you, Ian," Rory growled, feeling murderous. "I don't care if you're my brother or not. You'll need a fucking ambulance when I'm done."

"But you *don't* love her," Ian mocked from his perch.

"I don't want to talk about this!" yelled Rory, dragging his fingers through his hair in frustration. She was Brittany Manion. His teenage fantasy. An heiress. A woman who'd just gotten out of a shitty relationship. The last thing she needed was Rory making a move on her.

"Fine with me," said Ian, climbing back down the

ladder for another strand of lights. "We'll stop talking about it...as soon as you admit you love her."

"I don't even—"

"ADMIT IT!" bellowed Ian, his voice reverberating off the old barn walls as he stepped forward into Rory's space, chest to chest with his brother.

"Christ!" shouted Rory, flattening his hands on his brother's chest and shoving so hard that Ian stumbled backward. "You pushy *fuck*! *Of course* I fucking love her...much good it'll do me!"

"*Yes*!" Ian pumped one triumphant fist in victory. "I *knew* it. I fucking *knew* it."

All of the piss drained from Rory, and he leaned back against a wooden column, closing his eyes and shaking his head. He loved her. He loved Brittany Manion.

Well, of course he bloody did. He'd fallen in love with her the night he came home from Tierney's to find her curled up on his couch in the firelight. All he'd wanted from that day forward was...her.

"She's vulnerable."

"She's tougher than you think," said Ian, climbing back up the ladder.

"June said to fight for her," said Rory, opening his eyes.

"Isn't that exactly what you're doing?"

"No, Ian. Unless you hadn't noticed, I'm not doing *anything*! I'm standing around, counting down the days until she fucking leaves!"

"Wrong." Ian turned to face Rory, his usually jovial expression tightening. "You're not standing around doing nothing. You're here. You're giving her a place. You're giving her space. You're letting her know that she's beautiful and sexy and wanted. Rory, you're a dumbass if you think all fights require fists and fury. Some fights are quiet, but the battle's still being waged. Look at me: I'm fighting every single day of my life to stay clean." He gave Rory that same shit-eating grin before turning back around to wind the lights around the rafter over his head. "You're fighting too. You're fighting for her."

"Doesn't feel like it."

"The first step," said Ian, borrowing a line from AA, and using his most patronizing tone, "is admitting that you have a problem."

Rory crossed his arms over his chest, watching his brother work. His body was still hard and aching from his dance with Britt, and his heart was in deep chaos. Frankly, he was feeling pissed off in general. "Loving her is my *problem*, huh?"

"No, man. Loving her is awesome," said Ian. "It's only a problem if you deny it or try to hide from it. Because then you're not giving it a chance."

"I'm not denying it," said Rory softly. "I love her. I've probably loved her since I was fourteen. I've definitely loved her since the day she walked back into my life, looking for a place to marry another man. But what do I have to offer her?"

"I should deck you for asking such a stupid question."

"I'm serious, Ian. What have I got? An old camp? A dilapidated apartment over an old office building?"

Ian's voice took on a wistful quality. "You were always the good one, Rory. The smart one. The one who took care of the rest of us. The man with the plan. No matter what shit we were in, one look at Rory and we knew that everything would be okay in the end. You take care of people, and more than anything, that's what Brittany Manion needs. She's got houses and money and cars and hotels, but all that bullshit hasn't made her happy. She needs *you*, man."

"I don't know…"

"You're the heart of *trí ciarde*. You know that, don't you? I've had a lot of time to think about this, Rory, and *you're* the heart of us."

"What's Tierney?" asked Rory.

"The soul," Ian answered in total seriousness.

Realizing that this cuckoo analysis of their sibling bond was important to his brother, he swallowed his laughter. "Fair enough. What does that make you?"

Ian shrugged, offering Rory a crooked smile. "The entertainment?"

Rory laughed softly then, shaking his head at Ian. But his amusement was short-lived, his thoughts sliding seamlessly back to Brittany. "If I push her too soon, I could end up pushing her away. I don't want that."

"There are no guarantees, brother," said Ian, "but I'll keep fighting for my sobriety, and you keep fighting for Britt. And hopefully, at the end, I'll be standing sober…and you'll be standing next to your woman."

Ian went back to his work, and Rory whispered under his breath, more to himself than to Ian,

"May it be fucking so."

As she walked back through the woods, with her cheeks burning and belly fluttering like mad, Brittany couldn't help

but wonder:

What would have happened if Ian hadn't interrupted?

Would Rory have kissed me?

She quickened her pace, following the path back toward the office, trying to get her thoughts, and her still-trembling body, under control.

Yes, she decided. *He would have.*

And would she have let him?

The answer came quickly: *Hell, yes.*

Which clued her into something else—something she hadn't been completely aware of yet:

I'm over Ben. Absolutely. Completely.

Smiling to herself as the office came into view, she turned right onto the main path, following it down to Oxford Row.

Was she still hurt by what Ben did? Sure. When she was eighty years old and looked back on Ben's behavior, it might still sting that he'd treated her so badly. But during her weeks at Summerhaven, that hurt had been processed and cataloged. It was part of her past now. It wasn't active. It wasn't alive anymore.

She sucked in a deep breath of cool, clean mountain air and laughed softly to herself as Lady Margaret came into view. She was free of Travis. She was free of Ben. She was...free. It was like a terrible weight had been lifted from her shoulders.

Furthermore, for the first time in years, she realized that she had no plan for her future, but found she was okay with that too. It was okay not to have the next twenty years planned out. It was okay to see what life had in store for her without trying to manipulate it to her liking. In fact, she was finding that when she stopped planning, marvelous things happened—like coming to Summerhaven, like meeting new people and making new friends, and falling for Rory Haven...

She stopped short in front of her cottage.

"Falling for Rory Haven," she said aloud, her voice breathing life into the words. "Falling...for Rory. Oh, my God. I'm falling for Rory."

As she let the words find a place in her heart, she unlocked the door to her cottage and stepped inside. Flicking on the lights, she flopped back onto the bed, remembering how it felt to dance with him—his hard body pressed against hers, his voice soft near her ear, the skin on the back of his neck hot under her fingertips, his dark hair like silk. Her stomach filled with butterflies and she clenched her thighs together to quell the throb between them. Sighing with pleasure, she closed her eyes against the marvelous whirling feeling of wanting and being wanted.

She hadn't been certain about the intentions behind Rory's teasing comments and flirtatious looks, but now she was. He was interested in her. She was sure of it.

But it made a new question rise to the forefront of her mind: What, exactly, was he interested in?

A fling? Something sweet and casual?

Or something deeper altogether?

Brittany rolled to her side, looking out the window at the moonlight shimmering on the lake.

She wished she was the sort of girl who could have a fling. It would be so easy to offer herself to him if she was. She could even imagine the words tumbling from her lips: *I'm not looking for anything serious either, but I'm always up for fun!*

She bent her elbow, resting her head on her arm with a sigh.

The problem was that Brittany *wasn't* the sort of girl who had flings. And as much as she wished it wasn't so, her heart was already involved in this equation. She had *feelings* for Rory—she was already falling in love with him.

And while she knew that he was attracted to her, and he was certainly very kind to her, she didn't know if he was interested in something serious with her.

Until I know, she thought wistfully, her eyes fluttering closed, *I'd better protect my heart.*

When Brittany woke up the next morning, it was with a renewed sense of purpose. She spent the sunny morning gathering wildflowers from all over Summerhaven before taking armfuls to the kitchen, where Jamie let her set up a little assembly line to make up her vases. Packing the completed arrangements into empty produce boxes, she loaded them into the back of a golf cart and stopped by the office to pick up the ghost key that opened all the Oxford Row cottages.

"Good morning, dear!" greeted Mrs. Toffle. She picked up her newest read, *53 Letters for My Lover*, and flashed it at Brittany. "Have you started yet?"

"Not yet," said Brittany, "but I can't wait. I'm just sad that Ms. Attar doesn't have any more books for us to read."

"Yet!" cautioned Mrs. Toffle. "I stalk her on the Facebook. She's writing something new!"

The walkie-talkie on Mrs. Toffle's desk screeched and

she picked it up. "Mrs. Toffle here. Over."

Brittany couldn't help the smile that spread across her face when she heard Rory's voice. "Mrs. T, was Trinity supposed to be configured as two twins or one king?"

"I will check. Over. Hmm…" Mrs. Toffle looked up at Brittany thoughtfully before shuffling through the papers on her desk. "You look lovely today, my dear."

"Thank you."

"Like you're all lit up from inside."

"Oh, I…"

"Here it is." Mrs. Toffle picked up the walkie-talkie. "Two twins for Garrison and Hugh Carroll. Grandsons, I think. Over."

"Thanks, Mrs. T," answered Rory.

Mrs. Toffle set the walkie-talkie back in its charger before glancing up at Brittany again. "He's not seeing anyone, you know. He was, but now he's not."

She blinked at the older lady. "What? I didn't—"

"Oh, I know you didn't ask. I just thought you might want to know." She straightened the reservations. "He also dated someone in college, but it wasn't serious. I don't believe there's ever been someone serious in Rory's life."

Brittany told her mouth to say "How interesting. Have a nice day" and begged her feet to move, but neither obeyed. She just stood at the counter, watching Mrs. Toffle straighten up her desk, hoping for more covert information.

"Oh?" she prompted.

"He had big dreams, you know, of starting a chain of camps like Summerhaven. Graduated at the top of his class. Cornell. That's Ivy League. Yes. He even had funding lined up from some bigwigs in New York City. But then Colleen had her stroke, and Ted wouldn't leave her side. It was either shut the gates of Summerhaven, or…" She sighed.

"Wait. A chain of camps?" asked Brittany.

"Mm-hm. Conference center camps. For business-minded city folks to have retreats and such."

Brittany's mind processed this idea quickly, and it only took a minute for her to realize that it was a solid business plan. Strategically placed within an hour or two of major cities, conference centers based on Summerhaven's model could be a successful venture. No wonder he'd had funding lined up. Nobody was offering this, but there was a definite market for it.

"So…what happened?"

"He made the responsible choice and gave up his dream. He came home and took over the running of Summerhaven. Oh, he implemented some of his ideas here, but he didn't have time to start a new business while keeping this one afloat."

"Oh," murmured Brittany, her heart aching for Rory. She knew something about giving up on the dreams closest to her heart, and she was sorry he'd had to do the same. Not that she was surprised. For Rory—and all of the Havens—family would always come first. Never, in her whole life, had she met a man who had his priorities so well defined. It made her feel safe most of the time. Except for now. Right now it made her feel sad. "That's too bad."

"He's a good man," said Mrs. Toffle, looking up from her desk to meet Brittany's eyes. "The best. He'd do anything for his family…for the people he loves."

"I know that," said Brittany, thinking about the first day she'd come back to Summerhaven and how Rory had left a conference to her care so that he could help Tierney with Ian.

"Well, dear," said Mrs. Toffle, ending their conversation, "that group's coming in a few hours. Work to do. I'm sure you understand."

"Of course." Brittany straightened, taking a step away from the counter. "Thanks, Mrs. Toffle."

"He'd never have told you, dear."

Brittany turned back around. "What do you mean?"

"I've worked for the Havens since before Rory was born, and I know that man inside and out."

"I'm still not following you, Mrs.—"

"Rory would never let down someone he loves. Never risk hurting them. Never. As I told you, he'd give up his own dreams before he'd let that happen."

…someone he loves.

Was Mrs. Toffle suggesting that Rory loved her? And that he hadn't shared his plans with her because knowledge of them could somehow hurt her? Before she could process such an outlandish, breathtaking idea, the phone rang, and Mrs. Toffle answered it with a chipper, "Good morning! Summerhaven Conference Center!"

Her thoughts swirling in her head, Brittany reviewed Mrs. Toffle's words as she stepped through the screen door and onto the office porch. As she stood in the spring sunshine, clutching the ghost key for Oxford Row in her hand, her own words, shared with Rory weeks ago, rushed back to her:

Some men are intimidated by it—the name, the money, the hotels, the fame—and others just want to use you.

That was it.

In her bones, she knew it.

That's what Mrs. Toffle was trying to say: if Brittany and Rory ever got together, he'd give up on his dreams before he'd let her believe—even for a moment—that he'd used her to make them happen.

The flowers Brittany had arranged and placed in the cottages yesterday were a wonderful touch, mused Rory, though he hadn't had a chance to thank her yet. Between the check-ins yesterday and dinner last night, followed by a campfire with s'mores, Rory had been too busy to do more than wave at her as they passed on the main path.

Today was just as busy.

In addition to a buffet breakfast and barbecue lunch, the Carrolls had hired a hay wagon for rides around the camp, and Sven and Klaus were leading some of the older grandchildren and great-grandchildren on the ropes course. The dinner dance tonight required the setup of rentals in the barn, and when the bartender canceled at the last minute, Rory had to ask Doug to step in.

By the time nine o'clock rolled around, Rory stood outside the barn, exhausted but gratified, watching Carrolls of all ages dancing to music of the 1950s while tipsy revelers occasionally stepped up to a microphone to make an impromptu toast.

It had been a good weekend all in all, though he hadn't seen as much of Brittany as he would have liked. Then again, after their dance on Thursday night, maybe she needed a little space from him. The thing was, Rory really didn't want any space from her.

After admitting his feelings to Ian, he'd taken ownership of them quickly. He loved her. For the first time in his life, he was in love. And he was willing to walk the tightrope between what he wanted and how best to have it, because in the end—as Ian had said—Rory wanted to be standing with Brittany beside him.

"Hey!"

Looking over his shoulder, he was surprised to see the very object of his thoughts—dressed in jeans and a Summerhaven sweatshirt—approaching through the shadows of light cast by the lights they'd hung in the barn. Her blonde hair was back in a ponytail, and she looked so fresh and lovely, his heart lurched and stuttered.

I love her, it whispered. *I love you.*

"Hey," he said, holding out his hand to her.

She took it, lacing her fingers through his as she approached the barn to stand beside him. They stood side by side, connected by entwined fingers, watching in the darkness as the Carrolls celebrated a long and happy marriage.

"Sixty years," she said. "Isn't that something?"

"It is." Rory nodded. "You know, my parents have been together for thirty."

"Mine didn't even make it to five," she said ruefully.

"Their fate doesn't have to be yours. Maybe someday you'll be back here celebrating your sixtieth wedding anniversary, Britt."

She laughed softly beside him. "At the rate I'm going, I wouldn't bet on it."

It hurt him to hear her pick on herself, but he wasn't

sure how to make it better, so he squeezed her hand gently, hoping to convey that he was there for her, that he was on her side.

"Everything's gone great this weekend," she said.

When he glanced down, she was grinning at the festivities, her lovely face lit by the lights they'd hung up together. His heart filled with so much love for her, he was surprised that it could still beat, still function. "Yeah. It's been good."

"You've been busy," she said, looking up at him.

They were still holding hands—for no reason at all except that they felt like it, that they wanted to. He was so aware of the softness of her palm pressed against the callouses on his, he almost couldn't concentrate on their small talk. The skin-to-skin contact made his heart thrum, made his mind go wild, thinking of other, more intimate skin-to-skin contact he'd like to have with her. And he wondered what it meant to her—did holding hands mean that they were friends who liked each other? Or did it mean infinitely more to her, as it did to him?

"The work's a pleasure, though. I love groups like this one."

"I haven't asked you a lot about college," she said, "but you studied hospitality, right?"

"I did."

"You're very good at it, Rory. The changes you've made here at Summerhaven—they're wonderful. And the way you handle these groups is wonderful too. You have a knack for it."

In all of their conversations, he'd never told her about his plan to open a chain of Summerhaven-style camps across the country. He'd never want Brittany to suspect—even for a second—that his feelings for her were born out of her possible usefulness. She'd had enough disappointment from men: her father, her first husband, her latest fiancé. He didn't want a place on that list. Until he'd managed to present his ideas and get funding from one of the VC funds in Boston or New York, he didn't intend to ever mention it to her at all.

He squeezed her hand a little tighter. "I was sorry our dance got interrupted on Thursday night."

She gulped softly beside him. "Me too."

"I don't suppose you'd like to...." He bit his bottom lip, taking the plunge and hoping like hell that his timing wasn't off. "Would you like to go out on a date with me?"

"A *real* date?" she asked. "Like, the romantic kind or the hanging-lights kind?"

"The romantic kind," he said, chuckling softly at the memory of her insisting that Thursday night wasn't a date.

"When?" she asked, and he knew her well enough by now to hear the warmth in her voice, the happiness that he so wanted for her.

"Monday night?" he asked. "I'm free if you are."

The guests would be gone by then, and he could focus all of his attention on Brittany.

"You know I am," she murmured. "And yes. I'd like that a lot."

A bolt of something awesome shot through him like lightning, and he felt electrified by the sensation.

She said yes. And right this second, *yes* was the best word in the whole wide world.

"Yeah?" he asked, stepping in front of her so that his

body was facing hers, blocking some of the light from the barn with his back.

"Yeah," she said, staring straight ahead at his throat as Sam Cooke's "You Send Me" started playing in the barn.

Reaching forward, he placed a finger under her chin and tilted her face up to his. Shiny and dark in the dim light, her eyes met his, her tongue darting out to wet her lips.

This time, he wasn't missing his chance to kiss her.

Cupping her cheek in his palm, he lowered his head, his nose nuzzling against hers. He breathed her in—the light scent of her vanilla shampoo, the tea with honey she must have had after dinner before walking over to the barn. Her breath hitched and held, and he encircled her waist with his arm, pulling her closer as his lips touched down on hers for the first time.

Honey and tea, sweet woman and requited longing. The softness of her lips beneath his as he brushed his softly over hers. Her fingers unclasped his, sliding up his bare arm and sending shivers down his spine. Her other hand met its mate at the back of his neck, and she laced them together, holding him closer and urging him to deepen the kiss.

Wrapping both arms around her, he slid his tongue into her mouth, seeking hers, groaning softly when she answered his silent plea. She whimpered into his mouth, her back arching as he tilted his head the other way, sealing his mouth over hers again. Their tongues danced in sensual rhythm until the song neared its end and they drew apart from one another breathlessly.

"I wanted to do that on Thursday night," he said, the words gritty with emotion as he gazed into her eyes. "God, Britt, I wanted to do that so badly."

"Me too," she sighed, resting her head on his shoulder, her body molded perfectly to his.

The rocked back and forth to the last strains of "You Send Me," still holding each other when the music ended.

"Was it worth the wait?" she whispered, her voice warm and sweet, her breath dusting the base of his throat.

"Yeah, it was," he murmured, his heart beating wildly against hers. "It's late. I should get you home."

When the music switched to something upbeat, Rory stepped away from her, keeping her hand in his as he steered them toward the path in the woods that led to the office. They didn't speak much on the walk back to Lady Margaret, but Rory felt the fullness of his heart as she walked beside him, the promise of their upcoming date doing crazy things to his insides.

When they reached her door, they stopped in front of each other, with Rory looking down at her upturned face.

"I keep having these flashbacks to being a teenager," he said.

"We never did any of this when we were kids."

"We did in my dreams," he admitted. *Fuck, that was cheesy.* But then Britt made it all better by confessing:

"Mine too."

He grimaced. "I'm dying to kiss you again, but if I do, I'll want to stay for hours and kiss you all night long. And unfortunately, I need to get back to the Carrolls."

She smiled at him, her face luminous in the moonlight. "What time on Monday?"

"I'll pick you up at six?"

She nodded, pulling her key from her hip pocket. "Perfect."

"Night, Britt. *Mo mhuirnín.*"

"Good night, Rory," she whispered.

Turning to leave, he walked a short distance away from her cottage before whipping back around and covering the space between them. He grabbed her by the waist and hauled her up against his body before she could disappear inside. Dropping his lips to hers hungrily, he captured them in a fierce, wild kiss.

Her arms were trapped between them, her hands on his chest, but her fingers curled into his shirt as the kiss deepened, as he explored the hidden recesses of her sweet mouth, claiming them and making them his. She moaned her pleasure, and Rory reached for her ass, lifting her against the door, groaning when she wrapped her legs around his waist.

She tangled her hands in his hair, arching her back so that her breasts rubbed against his chest, wild images of her naked making him so hard that there was no way for her to mistake his arousal between them.

She whimpered into his mouth, slowing their kiss while sliding her hands to his cheeks and palming his face tenderly. She smiled at him, her lips red and slick, her eyes drugged and deep.

"Rory," she whispered, feathering her lips along his jawline to his throat where she kissed his throbbing pulse before pressing her lips to his one last time. When she drew back and spoke, her voice was breathless and needy. "I want you to stay...but I know you should go."

"Monday," he murmured, hating all the seconds between now and then.

Slowly, he loosened his grip on her so that she slid down his body, though he kept his hands on her waist until her feet touched the ground. Only when she was standing on her own did he let go and take a step back from her.

"Good night."

Her chest rose and fell quickly as she waved good-bye, leaning back against the cottage door as he disappeared into the darkness.

chapter thirteen

"So, you mean to tell me that you're holding my ice cream hostage?" asked Brittany, giving Rory what she hoped was a very disapproving look.

He grinned at her with a devilish gleam in his eyes. "Yep. And you don't get it until you kiss me."

"Are there no levels of deprivation you won't stoop to?"

"For a kiss? From you? Hmm." His lips twitched and he squinted his eyes as though in deep thought. Finally he shook his head. "Nope. I'm pretty much willing to do anything."

She giggled, then bit her bottom lip to keep from smiling. "Well...I do *love* ice cream."

"And it's your favorite flavor too," he said nonchalantly, blocking the TV show they'd been watching as he stood in front of her with two bowls of cookies and cream.

"Giffords?"

He scoffed like she was being ridiculous. "We're in New England. Is there any other kind?"

Unable to hold back her smile anymore, she uncurled herself from her cozy position on his couch and took the two bowls from his hands. She set them down on the coffee table, then wound her arms around Rory's neck, looking deeply into his eyes.

"Want to know something true, Rory Haven?"

His arms encircled her, holding her close, his eyes darkening as they looked into hers. "Yep."

"I like you more than Giffords cookies and cream."

He licked his lips, his eyes alighting on her mouth and lingering. "Is that a fact, Brittany Manion?"

"Mm-hm," she purred. "In fact…" She leaned up on tiptoes and kissed his right cheek. "I like you more"—she drew back only to press her lips to his left—"than anything."

His arms tightened around her as his mouth crashed down on hers possessively, claiming her fiercely, completely, his tongue meeting hers with a practiced sweep that came from the dozens of kisses they'd shared since Saturday night and their date on Monday. Brittany melted against him, the hard wall of his chest pushing against the softness of her breasts, a low sound of longing rumbling up from her throat. If she thought that she'd experienced happiness prior to this week, she knew it was only a crumb compared to the feast before her now. He had shifted the entire tilt of her world on its axis, and she saw everything from a different angle than before, like she'd been reborn or reprogrammed, like she'd never truly known how it felt to be loved before now.

His fingers curled into fists on her lower back and she arched against him, leaning her head to the side so that his lips could blaze a trail down the column of her throat, making her shiver with want. She threaded her fingers through the silk of his thick, dark hair, inhaling sharply when he sucked her ear lobe between his teeth and bit gently before claiming her lips again.

Finally he drew back, pressing his lips to her forehead before pulling her against him. His voice rumbled, low and thick with emotion, when he said, "I'm mad for you, Britt."

Tears pricked the back of her eyes and she blinked them rapidly, taking a deep breath and holding it until they subsided. She didn't want to cry; it's just that when he said something like that—so earnestly, so devotedly—her heart almost couldn't take it.

On Monday night, he'd picked her up at six as promised and taken her to dinner and a movie in nearby Meredith. Even now, she had no idea what she'd eaten or what movie they'd seen—every moment had been filled with an acute awareness of *Rory*, of being with him, of being…*his*.

She watched the eyes of other women in the restaurant as they looked him up and down, then slid their envious gazes to her. She memorized the way his eyes shined when he told her stories about his childhood adventures with Ian and Tierney. She loved the way his hand reached for hers as they walked from the restaurant to the movie theater, and when he put his arm around her in the dark theater, gently stroking her shoulder, she'd barely been able to concentrate on the plot.

Later, when they arrived back at Summerhaven, he'd invited her to his apartment for a cup of coffee, but they'd barely made it through the door before their hands were on each other, his lips slamming into hers in a bruising, desperate kiss, and her nails digging into his back as she pulled him closer.

"What are you thinking about?" he murmured, his hands gently massaging her back through her shirt.

"Monday."

"Good thoughts?"

"The best," she sighed.

He kissed the top of her head. "Our ice cream is melting."

But she closed her eyes and refused to unlink her hands behind his neck. "Let it."

Swooping her up in his arms, he circled the coffee table and sat down on the couch with her in his lap. He smiled at her, into her eyes, in a way that made her feel like she was the only woman on the earth, in the universe.

"How did this happen?" he asked, his expression filled with wonder.

She grinned up at him. "The question is…why didn't it happen sooner? We've known each other for thirteen years."

"Maybe we weren't ready for each other yet."

"Hmm. I needed to be dumped by Travis and Ben first?" she asked with a scoff. "Lucky me." She tilted her head to the side, looking up at him from her comfortable nest on his lap. "How about you? You know all about my disastrous relationships, but you never talk about previous girlfriends. I'm at a disadvantage."

He took a deep breath, leaning over her to grab the bowls and hand one to her. "Eat your ice cream."

"Are you avoiding the question?"

"No," he said, taking a huge bite. "I'ust'don'twannatalk'boutothergirlswi'you."

She sighed with pleasure as she took a bite of the semimelted ice cream. Lord, it was delicious. "I don't want *details*, Rory. Just an overview."

He pursed his lips, digging his heels in. "No good can come from discussing exes."

"Oh, really? Because *I've* laid my heart bare," she said. "And I don't even know if you *have* exes. It's not fair."

"I have exes," he acquiesced. "Not many, but I have them. Some. A couple."

"From college?" she asked, letting more melted cream slip down her throat.

"I dated someone in college, yes."

"Seriously?"

He shrugged, taking another bite. "Exclusively. So, yeah, I guess it was serious for college."

"How long?"

"Two years."

Her eyes widened. "That definitely sounds serious."

"We were eighteen when we met," he said. "When I was twenty, I went to Ireland for a year and studied abroad. She went to Japan to do the same. That was the end of that."

"You didn't try to make it work?"

He took a deep breath and sighed. "It wasn't practical. We, literally, didn't see each other for a full year. And when we met up with each other again at college senior year, we'd both changed. Moved on."

"Nobody special in Ireland?"

"I went on dates, but no. No one special."

Hmm. She didn't speak "Rory" well enough to know exactly what a "date" was. Did that mean he had casual sex with a bunch of girls in Dublin? Or that he actually went on dates to dinner and such?

"Serious dates?"

"Mostly forgettable dates," he said, finishing his ice cream and leaning over her to place his bowl back on the table.

"How about after college?" she asked.

"During my six glamorous years as the manager of Summerhaven?"

"No cutie across the lake for bootie calls?" she teased.

He froze and his eyes searched hers for a moment. "What do you mean by that?"

She giggled. "I'm just kidding. It's all family money and summer rentals on that side of Squam."

"Right," he said, smiling at her and nodding.

"So…no one special, huh?"

"Not as special as you," he answered, taking her bowl away and putting it on the table.

His eyes darkened when he leaned back and Brittany placed her hands on his shoulders, shifting on his lap to straddle him. He sucked in a sharp breath, his dark eyes focused on hers as his hands dropped to her hips. Experimentally, she shifted forward, grinding gently against him. His tongue darted out to lick his lips and his hands on her hips urged her forward again. Her heart thundered in her ears as she was pulled flush against him. He was hard under his flannel pants, the thin layer of soft cotton riding up around his erection as she surged forward once more.

For all that they'd spent every evening together this week, having dinner, kissing and making out over their clothes, they hadn't been naked with each other yet. Nor had they spent a whole night with each other, though they'd dozed off spooned together on the couch twice. Both times he woke her before dawn and walked her back to her cottage before the rest of the camp awakened or arrived for work; a little old-fashioned gallantry that she appreciated very much.

But after three nights of exploring what they could with

clothes *on*, part of her ached to take some *off*.

She moved against him again, and Rory's body, which was muscular and toned, flexed and hardened for her. His cock, bulging in his pants, left no doubt as to his arousal as she teased him, shifting forward again.

"Kiss me," he growled softly, his eyes dark and dilated, his fingers digging into the flesh of her hips.

She cupped his face, dropping her lips to his and gasping when he pulled her flush against his stiff cock, grinding it into the apex of her thighs. Trembling with desire, she reached for the hem of his shirt and pulled it over his head, then reached for her own and did the same. Wearing only a white lace satin bra, she rubbed her breasts against his bare chest, sighing with relief when she felt his fingers slide up her back and reach for the clasp. He opened the three hooks with a twist of his fingers, and she felt the elastic loosen, the ends drooping down at her sides.

Leaning back, she held his eyes, reaching for the strap on one shoulder and sliding it down her arm before reaching for the other. Rory reached forward and pulled the bra from her body, his eyes never leaving hers as he placed it on the couch beside them.

"Is this okay?" he murmured reverently as his hands skimmed up her sides to cup her naked breasts.

"This is perfect," she whispered, her breath hitching as he finally lowered his head to look at her.

He dipped his mouth to suck one pert nipple between his lips, circling his tongue around the pebbled flesh. Brittany reached up to cup the back of his head and guide his movements, whimpering her pleasure as he caressed her with his mouth and tongue, his soft lips and hot breath.

Yielding to him completely, she let her head fall back and closed her eyes, lost in a swirling that started in her stomach, taking her up, up, up until she was straining against him, her pulsing core flush against his throbbing erection.

"Rory," she cried, "it's too much. No more!"

His lips trailed slowly to the valley between her breasts, resting there, pressed against her shivering flesh as she cradled his head to her heart.

Panting with the soft waves of her small, unexpected orgasm, coupled with her ever-deepening feelings for him, she felt overwhelmed. And as though he knew, or sensed the reassurance she needed, he shifted her on his lap, cradling her in his arms. Relaxing against him, she rested her head on his shoulder and closed her eyes.

This is love.

This is what love really *feels like.*

Her words before, *I like you better than anything*, weren't accurate at all. As his strong heart beat quickly under her ear, she recognized the truth of her feelings in a startling wave of certainty:

I'm in love with Rory Haven.

I never laughed with Ben. I never cried with Ben. I was so scared of pushing him away, I couldn't be myself. But when I'm with Rory, I'm here, I'm with him, in the moment, aware of every breath, every sound, every touch, every feeling. I'm present. And I'm genuine. I laugh and I cry and I'm not scared that he'll push me away, so I don't hold anything back from him—I'm myself. I'm me.

This *is what love is.*

Rory took a deep breath, his chest pushing gently against her, and she looked up into his eyes, wondering if he could read the new tenderness in hers. He smiled at her, his expression surprisingly satisfied for a man who'd had relatively little satisfaction tonight.

"What?" he asked, searching her face like he was trying to memorize it for the hundredth time.

"You," she murmured. "You're wonderful."

He took a deep breath and sighed, reaching around her for her T-shirt. "Arms up."

"Why? You getting rid of me?" she asked.

"Nope," he said, working the sleeves over her raised hands, then giving her nipple a quick and final kiss before pulling the shirt down over her breasts. "Wherever I am, you're welcome."

"I know," she said, "that's the miracle of you."

"No, *mo mhuirnín*. That's the miracle of *you*...wanting to be here with me." He dropped his lips to her throat and pressed them to her pulse. "For the record, 'getting rid of you' isn't in my wheelhouse. I don't think forever would be long enough to learn the angles and contours of you...but I don't want to rush you or push you either."

"You're not," she said, though truthfully, she was a bit overwhelmed—in a good way—by what they'd shared tonight, coupled with the realization of her feelings for him. And with his usual intuitiveness, he just seemed to know.

She leaned forward, pressing her lips to chest, her hands wandering over *his* angles and contours. Drawing back, she grinned up at him. "But you'd better put your own shirt on, or I might not be able to control myself."

He chuckled, picking her up from his lap and depositing her on the couch beside him. Then he leaned down and grabbed his shirt off the floor, putting it over his head.

"I can't believe next Monday is Memorial Day."

Rory nodded. "And the camp open house."

"What's that?"

"Kind of a party. We invite all the locals from the surrounding towns to come swim in the lake and use the tennis courts and ropes course for free. We bring out the grills and make hot dogs and hamburgers for everyone. Doug sets off fireworks before folks go home. It fosters good will in the community."

"Sounds fun!" said Brittany.

"It is," he said, "especially this year...with you here." He caught his bottom lip between his teeth, his forehead furrowing.

"I know that look," said Brittany. "What's wrong? Spill it."

"I know you only booked Lady Margaret until Memorial Day, but it's free until June 3. You could stay if you want to."

Her heart clutched. June 3 was only ten days away. Was this Rory reminding her that time was coming for her to be moving on? Had she misjudged what was blossoming between them?

"Then I guess I'll stay until the third," she murmured, scanning his face.

His grimace deepened, and he sighed. "Yeah. Great."

"I mean, as long as you want me to..."

"Definitely," said Rory. "Stay until the third."

But the third felt too close when the only place on earth she wanted to be was with Rory. Was she supposed to leave Summerhaven in ten days? Go back to Boston? The thought made her stomach clench. She didn't want to go back "home." The only home she wanted was here, at Summerhaven, with Rory. How were they supposed to keep their new relationship growing if they were a hundred miles apart?

"I guess I'll head home," she said softly, standing up and snatching her bra form the couch.

"No!" said Rory. "We can still watch TV. We can—Britt, stay…"

"It's okay. I'm really tired," she said, forcing a brave smile as she hurried to the apartment door and wishing she had the courage to tell him that she wanted to stay a lot longer than June 3.

The following night, Brittany headed to dinner and book club with Mrs. Toffle, and Rory was left alone without her for the first evening since Monday. Grouching around his apartment, he was disgusted by how much he missed her, but even more, he was seriously out of sorts over the way things had wrapped up last night.

His intention had been to tell her that he didn't want her to go at all; not after Memorial Day and not after June 3. His intention had been to ask if she'd ever consider making Summerhaven her home—even if it was just for this summer, to test it out. His intention was to ask her to live with him, to stay with him, however she felt comfortable—in Tierney's room or sharing his—in a bid to get her to stay forever. Instead, it had all gotten muddled up, and all he'd done was shift her departure from May 28 to June 3, and it sucked. It wasn't what he wanted at all.

But everything between them was suddenly happening so fast. After mutual teenage crushes and a solid friendship that they'd been building for weeks, they were dating. No, it was much more than that. They weren't just dating; Rory was in love with her. And if his eyes didn't deceive him, her feelings for him were deepening by the day as well. But were they a couple yet? He didn't know for sure. And he didn't want to put pressure on her by asking her to put a name or definition on their new relationship, let alone ask her to uproot her entire life and stay with him.

But if he didn't suggest she move to New Hampshire, what was the alternative? Dating long distance? Commuting to Boston to see her once a week and hoping she'd do the same? He'd make the drive, and gladly, but he couldn't help worry that they'd lose the easiness and intimacy of the relationship they were building. And he didn't know how he could bear that. Because when he looked ahead at his future now, he saw Brittany in it.

A knock on his door made his heart lurch with hope that book group had been canceled, and he raced to the front of the apartment. When he pulled it open, he deflated like a balloon stabbed with a pin.

"Not who you were expecting, eh?" asked Tierney with one brow raised.

"More like, not who he was *hoping* for," said Ian, pushing passed Tierney and Rory to enter the apartment.

"What are you two doing here?" asked Rory, closing the door behind his siblings and following them inside.

"You and Britt missed dinner last night," said Ian, sitting down on the couch and putting his feet up on the coffee table.

Rory pushed them back onto the floor with a thud. "So what?"

"So you don't miss family dinners," said Tierney, sitting down next to Ian, "without a good reason. And if that good reason is what we think it is, we thought you should inform us."

"What are you two? My watchdogs?"

"Nope," said Ian. "Yer *dearthaireacha.*"

Siblings.

"*Tri ciarde*," said Tierney.

"With friends like you two..." said Rory, standing before them with his hands on his hips.

"So...?" prompted Ian. "Did what I interrupted last week finally happen?"

"A gentleman doesn't kiss and tell," said Rory, giving Ian a look. "Not that you'd know anything about that."

Tierney grinned. "So it's safe to assume you and Britt are an item now?"

"I don't know if it's *safe*," said Rory, sitting down on the coffee table across from them. "I can't figure out what happens next."

"What do you mean?" asked Ian. "You fuck like rabbits and—"

"Can you *not* be completely disgusting?" asked Tierney, elbowing Ian in the side.

"—and I was going to say, *before I was so rudely interrupted*—get down on one knee, get married, have a dozen babies, and live happily ever after."

Rory grinned. "That's not a bad plan...but don't you think it's a little premature? We've gone out on exactly one date."

"Pshaw!" exclaimed Tierney. "You've been circling each other for weeks. You're mad for each other, Rory. Anyone can see it."

"There are a few problems," said Rory pragmatically.

"Like…?"

"For one, she lives in Boston."

"Oh," said Tierney, "and no one in the history of mankind has ever moved for love."

"Me? Move to Boston?"

"I meant her moving here, but sure…you could move to Boston."

"*How*, exactly?" asked Rory, looking back and forth between his brother and sister and feeling defensive. "Abandon Summerhaven? Just toss up my hands and go along on my merry way? I'm not that selfish, and you know it. This place is everything to Mom and Dad."

Ian took a deep breath, leaning forward. "I could help more."

"No offense, Ian," said Rory, "but you've only been sober for a few weeks."

"No. I've been sober since April 1. Coming up on two months now," said Ian, lifting his chin. "And *no offense*, Rory, but you're not the only one who can run Summerhaven. I grew up here just like you. If you want time away from the camp to do something else, I think we should talk about how to make it happen."

Rory shifted his eyes to Tierney to get her take on this and was surprised to find her face open and engaged, like Ian's suggestion wasn't a terrible idea.

"He's right," she said. "He knows the ropes as well as you do. And we're not saying you should just jump ship. But

Ian could come on as comanager. Loosen up your schedule a little."

Rory weighed this possibility in his head. No, he didn't trust that Ian was prepared to suddenly run Summerhaven after two good months, but he did recognize that Ian had the skillset needed, and he had stayed sober for longer this time than any previous attempt. Giving Ian a chance to prove himself would also give Rory the time he needed to chase after his own dream. Hell, if he could get funding for his idea, he'd have something substantial to offer Brittany. He'd be a business owner, and yeah, he could eventually move to Boston so she wouldn't need to uproot *her* life.

The more he thought about it, the more excited he felt.

"You mean it?" he asked Ian.

Ian nodded. "Yeah. I've left you holding the bag for too long. I need to grow up, Rory. This place will help me do that."

"You'd need to come on as coassistant manager with Doug for this summer. And then in September, I could promote you to comanager," said Rory.

"Sounds good," said Ian, looking around their childhood home with appreciation. "I'll move in here with you next week."

"With *me*?" asked Rory, thinking about the recent nights he and Britt had spent on the couch, making out until dawn.

"Yeah," said Ian. "Where else would I go?"

Rory frowned at his brother, though he knew that Ian was right. Yes, there was another staff apartment on campus—a tiny loft over the chapel—but Ian's recovery was still too new for him to live alone. He still needed someone to keep an eye on him.

Tierney, reading Rory's mind, grinned at him. "Poor Rory. His love nest's being invaded."

"Enough of that," he told her, turning to Ian. "I'm glad to have you here, Ian. Thanks for offering."

"Thanks for saying yes, bro. I'm excited."

"Will you shave the beard?"

"Absolutely not," said Ian. "It would take someone prettier than you to get me to part with it."

"What'll you do with the extra time, Ror?" asked Tierney. "Try to get your idea up and running? What does Britt think about it?"

"Yes," said Rory, nodding at his sister. "I'll get the business plan out, update it and polish it. Maybe I'll reach out to Professor Collins and see if he'd be willing to set up those meetings in New York for me again."

"And Britt?" asked Tierney, like a dog with a bone. "She loved the idea, right?"

Rory looked away from his siblings. "I haven't told her."

"Why not?" asked Ian. "With her connections, she could give you a hand."

"That's just it," said Rory. "I don't want a hand...not from her. I don't ever want her to think that I got together with her just so that I could get a leg up in the hospitality business. In fact, I'm never telling her about it. Not until the day I have funding."

"Are you sure that's wise?" asked Tierney, cocking her head to the side. "Most women don't love it when things are kept from them, you know."

"Most women aren't Brittany Manion," he said. "What if she thought I was just after her money?"

Ian hooted with laughter. "Then she doesn't know you at all, boyo."

"Ian's right," said Tierney. "Anyone who knows you knows that'd be beneath your character."

"Either way, I won't risk her. I can't."

Tierney still looked troubled. "Just be sure you're not risking her by *withholding* it, huh?"

Rory was done talking about this. "Let me worry about it, huh?"

"Sure, Rory," she said, like she hoped he knew what he was doing.

"So…the party on Monday," said Ian, grinning at Rory. "Man, I love a party! Fill me in. Now that I'm assistant manager, I guess I'll have some real responsibilities around here." He nudged Tierney in the side. "You think the boss will give me a company car?"

"I think you'll be lucky if the boss doesn't give you a boot in the rear," said Tierney, laughing at her brother as the Haven triplets turned to the planning of Summerhaven's annual party.

CHAPTER FOURTEEN

Memorial Day arrived with bright-blue skies, and Brittany woke up to a beam of sunlight shining across her bed.

She stretched her arms over her head and groaned happily. Since Ian had moved into the apartment over the office last Friday, she and Rory had been hanging out in Lady Margaret. Last night, they'd spent some time going over the plans for the party today before falling asleep in each other's arms. He was gone this morning, of course, having slipped out before dawn. She turned her face into his pillow and breathed deeply, smelling him: pine and soap and Rory.

Though their conversation on Wednesday night had left her feeling a little insecure, she was grateful to have Thursday away from him to gain some perspective. What was he supposed to do? Ask her to move in with him and his brother? That would be awkward. Or leave Summerhaven and move to Boston to be with her? She hadn't made that offer to him, and it would have been presumptuous for him to suggest it. He was inviting her to stay for as long as possible before the summer season began, and at face value, that meant that they were maximizing the time they had together.

As for the future? Well, they'd have to talk about it.

And unlike Ben, with whom she'd avoided difficult conversations, she wouldn't avoid it with Rory. In fact, tonight, after the fireworks, she intended to bring it up.

Because weekends were his busiest time, she could volunteer to come up and see him on the weekends, and perhaps he could come down to Boston and spend one night a week at her place. More than anything, she trusted him— he'd never given her reason not to, and his transparency meant everything to her—and as long as they wanted their relationship to work, she trusted that they'd put the effort into making that happen.

Was she nervous? Of course. Her luck in the past hadn't exactly primed her confidence, but Rory was the most genuine, most loving, most trustworthy person she knew. If anyone on earth wouldn't let her down, it was him. She rolled out of bed and got dressed, ready to start a wonderful day at Summerhaven.

After running the carnival games all morning and sitting beside Farmer Hank in the front seat of the hay wagon, giving camp tours all afternoon, she was tired by early evening. Standing on the food line, waiting for a burger, she didn't notice Ian beside her until he tapped her on the shoulder.

"Hey, Britt!"

"Hey, trouble."

"Trouble? I'm hurt!" He pointed to the logo on his shirt. "Didn't you hear? I've gotten more responsible lately. In fact, Summerhaven's got a new assistant manager."

"I heard. Poor Summerhaven," she said, grinning up at Rory's brother, who looked so much better than he had two months ago at Tierney's house.

"Hope my promotion isn't cramping your style," he said, giving her a suggestive grin. "You know, hosting my brother in your little cottage night after night…"

"What happens in my little cottage night after night is none of your affair, boyo," she said, making him throw back his head with laughter.

When he stopped laughing, he nudged her in the hip. "Hey, you know…I've been meaning to ask you something."

"Oh, yeah?" she asked, nodding her thanks at the server who placed a fresh-off-the-grill burger on her waiting bun.

"Yeah. About Halcyon."

Brittany squeezed some ketchup on her plate and grabbed a handful of chips from a big bowl. "Forget it."

"Britt, come on," said Ian, following her to a nearby picnic table almost filled with locals happily gorging themselves on free barbecue. "Just tell me…how is she?"

"Last I heard? Terrible."

Ian grimaced, rubbing his beard. "Why? What else happened?"

"Her ex-husband racked up tens of thousands of dollars on her credit card. It's holding up the divorce. She thinks they may need to declare bankruptcy."

"Fuuuuck," muttered Ian.

"Yeah," said Britt, taking a big bite of her sandwich. She chewed slowly, watching Ian process this news.

"Bastard."

"Uh-huh," agreed Brittany, looking over Ian's shoulder for a glimpse of Rory. She'd barely seen him all day.

Suddenly she caught sight of him near the lemonade table. He was talking to a blonde woman with long hair who wore a tied-dyed sundress. From the looks of her, Brittany would guess she was in her forties, and from the Bulgari sunglasses she was wearing, she was obviously from money. "Hey, Ian...who's that? Who's Rory talking to?"

Ian looked over his shoulder, then turned back to Brittany, his expression guarded. "No one."

Brittany looked at the woman again, the way she reached out to touch Rory's arm, her fingers curling around his skin and lingering as she laughed at something he said.

"She's not *no one*," said Brittany, putting her burger down as her appetite disappeared completely, the memory of Ben and Angie in the hospital cafeteria flashing through her mind. "Who is she? What's her name?"

"She's just...she's a photographer who lives on the other side of the lake. Her name's June."

I just don't think June's right for your event.

June. She remembered Rory mentioning June. She was the photographer who he'd originally suggested to capture her wedding and then awkwardly *un*recommended after they'd spent a little more time together.

"Who is she?" whispered Brittany, a terrible ache taking hold of her. "I mean...who is she...to Rory?"

"I don't want to..." Ian held her eyes for a moment, then shifted his away. "Talk to Rory. He'll tell you. It's not my place...but, Britt? Believe me. It's nothing you need to be worried about."

Except Ian's body language didn't correspond with his claim that June was "nothing." He was evading the question and avoiding her eyes, and it made Brittany's blood run cold in recognition. *Secrets. Lies. Cheating.* She'd been here before.

"Fine," she said, picking up her plate and standing up from the table. Leaving Ian, she headed for the garbage can, throwing away most of her food.

"Hey, Brittany!" said Doug, who was passing her with a tray of watermelon slices.

She offered him the brightest smile she could muster. "Hey, Doug! Great party."

"Yeah," he said, looking around with a satisfied nod. "Everyone's having fun."

"Hey, Doug," she said, hooking her thumb in Rory's direction, and trying to sound casual, "how long ago did June and Rory break up?"

"Huh," said Doug, wrinkling his forehead. "Did they break it off? I didn't know."

"So they've been together for a while, huh?"

"Mmm. Together?" Doug grinned at her. "I don't know if I'd call them *together*, Britt. More just banging boots, I think."

"*Banging boots*," she murmured, feeling her heart drop to her stomach like a big, fat brick as tears welled in her eyes. "Right."

"Hey…are you okay?"

"Yeah! Dust in my eye. G-Great party, Doug," she said before hurrying away.

Beelining to the path in the woods, she power walked back to the main path, tears streaming down her cheeks as she panted from exertion and fury and sadness.

…*it's free until June 3. You could stay if you want to.*

But not beyond the third, right? Because there's another June across the lake waiting for some "boot banging" as soon as the fourth rolls around!

"Stupid, stupid, stupid," she muttered through tears, turning right onto the main path toward Lady Margaret.

Luckily all of the visitors were at the barbecue, and no one was around to see the crying crazy lady talking to herself. "Why would your luck change, dummy? Why would Rory be different? How many times does this need to happen before you see? Before you get it through your thick head? There's something *wrong* with you, Brittany! Face it! You're unlovable!"

Walking fast and not looking down, she tripped on a root, falling to the gravelly path with a cry as her hands broke her fall. When she turned them over, bloody and dirty, it only made her cry harder, and she stood up, pressing them to her pants. Then she continued her walk, slower now, all of her indignation swallowed by the stinging in her hands, by the anguish in her heart.

She'd thought Rory was different. She'd believed that he was special, that he wouldn't let her down. But here she was, bleeding and broken, as she pulled her suitcase out from under her bed and started throwing her clothes into it.

He had someone else—like Travis, like Ben. She wasn't enough for him, and she'd probably never be enough for any man. And it fucking hurt. It hurt because she wanted to belong to someone, and she thought she belonged to Rory. And damn, it, she loved him. She was madly and completely in love with him in a way that felt different from any man she'd loved before.

But it *wasn't* different.

It was just more of the same.

And Brittany Manion had finally had enough.

The look on Ian's face as he approached told Rory that something was going down…and that it wasn't good.

"Will you excuse me, June?"

"Of course. And Rory," she said, leaning forward to press a kiss to his cheek. "I'm happy for you. I'm glad it all worked out with Miss Impossible."

"Me too," said Rory, waving good-bye to her before meeting Ian halfway across the field. "What's up?"

"Brittany."

Rory froze, scanning Ian's face. "Is she hurt? What happened? Where is she?"

"Fuck," muttered Ian, rubbing the back of his neck. "Halfway back to Boston? She saw you with June. I didn't tell her who June was, but she knew something was up between you two. Then I saw her talking to Doug, and after that she took off."

"When?"

"Five minutes ago?"

"I was just *talking* to June! Nothing else."

"Yeah, but old lovers have a way of touching sometimes…a hand on an arm…the way you might lean in a little too close when you laugh. It's the leftover comfort of established intimacy…even if things are over…"

"Fuck," Rory growled. "Did it look that bad?"

"From where she was sitting?" Ian winced. "Didn't look good, man."

Rory handed his clipboard to Ian. "Take this. And don't come and find me unless the whole place is burning down."

"Yeah! Yeah. Don't worry! I've got things under control," called Ian at Rory's back. "You go after her!"

Racing through the woods, Rory didn't stop until he

reached the main path, panting as he speed walked the rest of the way to Lady Margaret.

Half of him was worried out of his mind, and the other half was furious.

He knew that she'd been hurt by other men, and he understood from Ian how his and June's body language—coupled, no doubt, with misinformation from Doug—had led her to believe he was cheating on her.

But, damn it, he'd done everything—*everything*—possible to make her feel safe, to prove himself to her, to move at her pace, and the idea that she would run off without even talking to him hurt. In fact, it made him fucking furious, and the idea of losing her scared him to death.

When he reached Lady Margaret, he could hear her banging around inside, doing God only knows what, but he was so grateful she was still there, he rested his hands on his knees for a moment and took a deep, calming breath.

Then he stepped over to the cottage and knocked on the door.

"Britt?"

"I'm…*not*…here!" she yelled.

"Let me in."

"Screw you!"

"Open up," he said. "June and me…it's not what you think."

She threw open the door, and Rory winced at the sight of her: red-rimmed eyes, wet cheeks and fists by her sides—she was barely holding herself together. *Shit. This is bad.*

"Britt," he said gently, hurting for her, "please let me in, *mo mhuirnín*. We need to talk."

211

"*Mo mhuirnín?* Your s-sweetheart?" she scoffed, her face crushed. She reached up to swipe away more tears. "Just how many *sweethearts* do you have, Rory?"

"One," he said, holding the door and stepping inside. "You. *Only* you."

"I don't believe you," she spat, turning back to her suitcase.

His eyes followed her motions, his whole body tensing up when he realized she was packing. He reached for her arm, forcing her to stop what she was doing, turn around, and face him.

"I *asked* if you dated anyone while you've been here," she cried.

"And I said, 'No one special.'"

"Well, it sure looked special to me!"

"Brittany, I'm *not* sleeping with June. I haven't slept with her since *before* the day you came to check out Summerhaven. I swear it on Tierney and Ian's lives. Once I'd met you again—even though you were engaged to another man—I ended things with June."

She was motionless, staring up at him, and he could feel the struggle within her. She wanted to believe him, but her past hurts were making it difficult for her to trust.

"I promise you, Brittany. I promise you that since the day you walked back into my life, there's been no one for me…but you."

"Why didn't you tell me about her?"

"Why *would* I? What man tells the woman he loves about some other woman?"

Her eyes widened and her lips parted in surprise. "Wait. What did you say?"

He was still holding her arm, but he slid his fingers down her arm to her hand, winding his fingers through hers, grateful that she didn't pull away. "I love you. And maybe it's too soon for me to tell you that. But, Britt…sweet woman…that's the truth. That's all my cards on the table. I love you."

"You…love me?" she asked, her body swaying toward him, though her feet didn't move.

"I've been in love with you since the day you walked back into my life looking for a place to get married. I'm crazy about you. Mad for you. Distracted. I keep having conversations with you in my head, trying to get you to consider staying for the summer, or—or, hell, *forever*, but I'm not good at this and I—"

"You're doing fine," she said softly, her face relaxing just a little as she squeezed his hand. "Keep going."

He stepped forward, closer to her, searching her eyes. "I'm not perfect, but I will *never* hurt you on purpose. I will never, ever cheat on you. I will never lie to you."

"What's the deal with you and June?" she asked, lifting her chin, her expression so desperate to trust him, it twisted his heart.

"We were…I don't know what you called it. Um, friends with benefits, maybe? We'd occasionally get together at her place for dinner or drinks and sometimes that led to…to…" He let his voice trail off.

"How long did this go on for?" she asked.

"A couple of years. Now and then. It wasn't a regular thing."

"Do you love her?"

"No! No, no, no! Not at all! It's not like that. Not even

a little. June's a *friend*. That's it."

"So she was your friendly booty call across the lake?" asked Brittany, pursing her lips in disapproval.

"Sort of. I guess." Christ, he hated this entire conversation. "But I'd give up her friendship forever if you asked me to."

"I wouldn't," she whispered. "I don't want you to give up friends for me."

"I swear to you—she and I were over the moment you walked back into my life. Can you trust me?"

She still looked a little worried and disapproving, but at least she wasn't crying anymore. Finally she took a deep breath and nodded. "I believe you, Rory. I trust you."

"Thank God." He felt the adrenaline begin to drain from his tense body. "It would kill me to lose you."

"You won't," she said, letting him pull her into his arms. "I'm yours."

"And I'm yours," he pledged. "I love you, Britt. I'm crazy in love with you."

She gulped, her brown eyes so wide, he couldn't look away as she whispered, her voice breathless and tender, "I love you too, Rory. That's why it hurt so much to think I'd misjudged you."

It was his turn to blink at her in shock, because never—not in his wildest, sweetest dreams—did he expect to hear those precious words from her so soon.

"Say it again," he murmured.

She smiled at him—a small smile, but after their fight, he needed it. He needed to know they were going to be okay.

"I love you," she said. "Is it too soon for me to fall in love again? I don't know and I don't care. I love you. That's how I feel, and there's nothing I can do about it. There's nothing I *want* to do about it…except to let it happen."

He couldn't stop himself from dropping his lips to hers in a passionate, relieved kiss, grateful when she reached up and locked her hands behind his neck, arching against him with a low moan. His blood sluiced hot and fast to his cock, which hardened under his khaki shorts, pressing its length into her, wanting her, needing her in ways they hadn't begun to explore.

Reaching for her cheeks, he leaned away from her so he could look into her eyes. There was something else he needed to say.

"I messed up on Wednesday night, Britt. I don't want you to leave on Sunday. I don't *ever* want you to leave. I just didn't want to put pressure on you. On us. This thing between us is still new. But if you want to stay, there's a little place over the chapel that's all yours. Ian and I can fix it up, and you can stay as long as you want." When she didn't answer, he scanned her face, looking for clues as to her feelings. "Or, um, if you need to go back to Boston, I'll come see you as much as I can. Every week. Ian's taking over more now, so I can take a few days off and drive down for a couple of nights. We'll make it work, Britt. God, please tell me you want to make it work too. Please."

She reached for his hands, covering them with hers. And as he stared down at her beloved face, he slowly realized the reason she hadn't answered yet was because her eyes were brimming with fresh tears. She sobbed softly, tightening her grip on his hands.

"Don't be sad," he said, leaning forward to nuzzle her nose, to brush his lips over hers.

"I'm not sad," she murmured, her lips moving softly against his. "I'm so happy, I don't know what to say."

His own happiness surged and he reached for her, lifting her into his arms. He held her tightly, kissing her relentlessly before pivoting toward the empty bed. Lowering her down to the duvet, he followed, lying on top of her, bracing his weight on his elbows as he kissed her. Her fingers slid down his back to his waist, pulling his polo shirt from his shorts, and he paused in kissing her to grab the shirt behind his neck, pull it over his head, and toss it on the floor. With Rory still straddling her hips, Britt sat up and did the same, her shirt landing softly on top of his.

"Are we doing this?" he murmured, his voice husky with need.

"I can't wait anymore," she answered, reaching behind her back to unclasp her bra and let the straps trail down her arms. "I trust you. I love you. I want you."

Pulling the pink satin from her chest, Rory gasped softly as his gaze dropped to the twin points of her pink nipples, standing at attention, ready for him. He lay down on his side and dipped his head, sucking one bud into his mouth and laving it with his tongue as she plunged her hands into his hair and whimpered. Skimming his lips to her other nipple, he circled the straining flesh with the tip of his tongue, around and around until the need to taste her overwhelmed him and he sucked the stiff nub between his lips.

She cried out, her breathing shallow and choppy, desperately forcing his head up and smashing her lips into his for a hungry kiss. Rory reached for the elastic waistband of her shorts, flattening his palm over the rutched fabric in case she wanted to stop him or slow down. But she responded by kissing him harder, so he slipped his thumbs under her panties and pulled them down to her ankles. He knelt beside her, gently clasping each foot to remove them entirely.

Naked on the bed with the afternoon sun bronzing her body, Brittany was so beautiful, he could barely believe that she was his—that he was allowed to love this goddess-woman, that she'd narrowly escaped the clutches of two unworthy men to somehow wind up with him.

"You're stunning," he whispered, his eyes resting on the smooth skin that hid her sex. His mouth watered. He wanted to taste her.

"Now you," she murmured, and his eyes slid slowly up her body, locking with her dark, steady gaze.

Backing up until he stood on the floor by the foot of the bed, he held her eyes as he unbuckled his belt, then reached for the button on his shorts, opening them quickly, hooking his thumbs under his boxers and shoving them down his legs. As naked as she, his cock jutted out form his body, pulsing with his every heartbeat, aching to be surrounded by the wet heat of Brittany's body. But first, he wanted to be sure she was ready for him.

Gently spreading her legs, he crawled up the bed, positioning himself between her thighs and flattening his hand over her mons. "Is this okay? If I touch you here?"

She nodded as one of his fingers slid between the lips of swollen flesh, his calloused digit swiping over her clit and eliciting a deep moan. She closed her eyes, leaning back in the pillow beneath her head as he traded his finger for his tongue. Cupping her ass, he pulled her body closer, burying his face in the apex of her thighs and sucking softly on her throbbing flesh.

The sounds of her moans and whimpers, coupled with the way her back rose off the bed with pleasure, made Rory's cock impossibly harder, straining and stuff, desperate to feel the soft, wet, heat of her sex around him. The fingers in his hair tugged and scratched, and finally he realized she was pushing him away.

"I want to feel you inside me," she murmured, her dark eyes cracking open to look down at him.

Me too. "Are you on the pill?"

She nodded. "Have you been careful?"

"I've always used condoms in the past, but…" One, he didn't want to stop what they were doing, get dressed, run home to get a condom, and then run back here…and two, he wanted to *feel* her. He wanted to feel *everything.*

"I don't want anything between us either," she said softly, reading his mind. Her sweet lips tilted up in a smile as she reached up and caressed his cheek. "Come to me, Rory. No more waiting."

He leaned down to kiss her, positioning his ready cock at the entrance of her sex, then pushed forward, slowly, carefully, locking his eyes with hers to watch her, to feel the intense intimacy of the moment as they joined their bodies together.

"I…love…you…" he panted, drawing back before thrusting forward into her sweetness again. And Brittany, who miraculously loved him back, met his movements with her own, receiving him, holding him, wanting him, and loving him.

And after they'd cried out each other's names and the

shudders of bliss had subsided, Rory held her limp, sated body against his own, thanking God and every angel that had ever safeguarded His creation that the woman of his deepest dreams was the realest gift he'd ever been given.

"We never finished our conversation," said Rory, holding her against his chest, his naked front to her naked back and a warm duvet around them both. "We got distracted."

They were sitting on the roof of Lady Margaret, watching the fireworks that Doug was setting off up the path near the north dining hall. It was a perfect view, a perfect celebration, a perfect end to the best day of her life.

He leaned down to press his lips to her bare shoulder. "No pressure, *mo mhuirnín*. I want *you* to decide what happens next."

"No," she said, sighing contently as she leaned back against him. "I've made enough solo plans in my life. It doesn't work. Any plans from now on, we make *together*."

"Okay," he said, trailing kisses along her collarbone before resting his chin on her shoulder. "Then here's what I want: I want you to stay with me at Summerhaven this summer. We'll fix up the apartment over the chapel, and it'll be yours. Well, *ours*. I'll go back and forth between your place and mine so I can still keep an eye on Ian."

"That sounds good to me," she said, smiling at the lake that held so many of her dearest memories from childhood and would be the sight of so many happy days with her love. "I'll need to go to Boston now and then to check on A Better Tomorrow. And there are occasional stockholder meetings at Manion International that I attend. I meet up with possible donors at benefits and galas, so I attend those sometimes as well…though I'd love it if you'd be my date when I got an invitation."

"You, in a dress and heals? Hell, yes, I'll be there."

She giggled softly. "And after the summer? What then?"

He took a deep breath. She knew that if she looked at him, he'd have that telltale crease in his forehead, but she also knew that she could trust him. Whatever was on his mind, he'd tell her when it was time.

"If Ian's doing well, we could talk about moving to Boston together someday."

"You'd do that?" she asked, turning slightly in his arms so she could see his eyes.

"Oh, yeah. I longed for Boston when I was kid. I longed for anywhere besides Summerhaven. I mean, don't get me wrong, I had a good childhood and I'll always love it here. But I wanted more than this camp in such a quiet town. Maybe this is my chance to have that."

"With me," she said, leaning forward to kiss him.

"*Always* with you," he answered, leaning his forehead against hers as fireworks lit up the night sky over Summerhaven.

chapter fifteen

Four Months Later

"Why won't you tell me where you're going?" asked Brittany, her blonde hair beautifully tousled and tan skin flushed from morning sex.

They'd woken up in her bed an hour ago, their naked bodies reaching for each other, still insatiable, though they'd spent every night together since Memorial Day.

"Because it's a surprise," he said, kissing her forehead before swinging his legs over the side of her bed. "Don't you trust me?"

The little apartment over the chapel, which included a bedroom / sitting room combination, tiny bathroom, and galley kitchen, had been the site of many unholy deeds this summer, thought Rory with a devilish grin. Though the ever-growing devotion between him and Brittany was so true and so strong, he couldn't imagine that a loving God would disapprove.

"You know I do," she said, a tinge of a whine in her voice. "I'm just being nosy."

"Well, Leylah Attar's newest book isn't going to read itself, *mo mhuirnín*, so I expect you'll keep busy."

He looked at her over his shoulder and smiled at her, wondering if he'd ever tire of the sight of Brittany Manion, naked in bed. He couldn't imagine a day when it wasn't his favorite image on earth.

"Yes," she agreed. "I can't wait to get started."

"And I'll be back tonight," he added.

"I know," she grumbled.

"Not to mention, you worked hard all summer, sweetheart. You deserve a few quiet days off now that the busy season's come and gone."

She took a deep breath and hummed softly as she let it go. "Mmmm. I guess so. But I'm sorry it's over already. It was the best summer ever, Rory."

"Yeah?"

"So much fun," she said, pushing the blanket down on purpose so that Rory could see her pink nipples. She reached for them, running one finger suggestively around each of the puckering buds until both stood at attention.

Damn, but she was the sexiest, most tempting woman on creation. His cock, still slick from their recent lovemaking, twitched with need, blood quickly pumping it back to its full length and width. He didn't need to leave for Boston *quite* yet, did he? His meeting wasn't until this afternoon.

"I want you," he murmured, pulling the blanket away from the rest of her body and rolling on top of her. She spread her legs and he slid into her hot, wet center, grunting his pleasure as she sheathed him, the walls of her sex holding him tight.

"I'm yours," she promised.

He leaned down and kissed her, his tongue sliding against hers as his hips retreated, then slid forward—slowly, so fucking slowly—once again.

"I love you," she said, rising to meet his slow, deep

thrusts.

"I love you more," he answered, kissing her again as he began to move faster, the friction they created them making them both sigh and moan as their pleasure built.

He cried out his release a moment after she did, emptying himself inside of her and resting his forehead on hers as their breath mingled in sharp, quick pants of exertion.

"Don't go," she said.

He kissed her nose, then withdrew from her warm body, missing her already. "I have to."

Determined not to be tempted by her again, he slipped out of bed and walked straight into her bathroom, turning on the shower and stepping inside the tiny stall as soon as the water was warm. Grabbing a bottle of body wash, he soaped his body, running his hands over the muscles he'd kept in good shape with a summer's worth of hard work in the books.

Ian had proven as good as his promises, now six months sober and officially the comanager of Summerhaven Conference Center. And Rory, who'd managed to update and polish his business plan from Cornell, was finally meeting with a venture capital firm in Boston today, hoping to get the funds he needed to make his dream a reality. And once he did?

Well, then he'd be ready to ask Brittany a question that had been sitting at the tip of his tongue for weeks. They could keep their tiny apartment at Summerhaven for weekends, or he could even have a cottage built for them somewhere on the property, but either way, they could move to Boston and start a whole new chapter of their life together.

But first, he needed that money.

He was counting on it.

It was the last missing piece of the finished puzzle he could already see in his mind, which included a wife and children he could provide for himself, even if—technically—he didn't *need* to.

He turned off the water and grabbed a towel from the hook behind the door, running it through his hair before wrapping it around his waist. He'd go back over to the office apartment to shave and get dressed, but first he wanted to spend a couple more minutes with his woman.

Opening the bathroom door, he found her sitting up in bed, counting something out on her fingers, a perplexed look on her face.

She turned to him, tilting her head to the side. "What's today's date?"

"September 30."

"Hmm," she said, biting on her bottom lip in thought.

"Why?" he asked, opening the top drawer of her dresser and pulling out a pair of clean boxers. "What happens today?"

She took a deep breath and brightened, smiling at him. "Nothing. It's easy to lose track of the days here."

"So…Leylah Attar and sunshine today?" he asked her, grabbing his jeans off the wicker rocking chair where he'd thrown them last night.

"Leylah Attar and sunshine," she said distractedly, looking out the window at the beautiful fall day.

"Are you certain?" asked Cheryl, Chef Jamie's wife, who'd become one of Brittany's closest friends over summer. They sat on the main dock in the sunshine, eating a picnic of pesto chicken salad and yucca chips that Jamie had delivered from the kitchen.

"It could be anything," said Brittany, rubbing her forehead with her thumb and forefinger. "Maybe I'm just miscounting. But I'm on the pill. I generally get it like clockwork on the twentieth of every month. So, yeah. I think it's late. Ten days late."

"If you're on the pill, how did this happen?"

"Remember when Rory came to Boston over Labor Day weekend and surprised me? I was there for the annual Manion gala, and he didn't think he could make it, but he showed up at the last minute? Remember?" She thought back to that night—to how dreamy Rory looked in a tuxedo, striding into the ballroom, his eyes on a search for her. And the way he'd looked at her once he'd found her? Swoon. Every woman in the room had wished she was Brittany.

"Of course! He borrowed Jamie's tux."

"My pills were *here*. I'd left them here by mistake. Forgotten them...and we—I don't know...one thing led to another. I didn't have condoms in my apartment." And they had practically ripped each other's clothes off when they'd gotten back to her place after the party.

Cheryl flashed her friend a worried look. "What are you going to do?"

It took Brittany a beat to understand what Cheryl was

asking. "Oh! Keep it, of course. I just…"

"What do you think Rory will say?"

She thought back to one of their first conversations when she asked if he wanted kids and he said, *Yeah, of course. I'm Irish. It's one of our specialties.*

But saying he wanted kids someday and having a baby next May were two different things. She bit her bottom lip. "Well, I hope that he'll…I mean, I hope he'll want it. The timing isn't perfect, but we love each other, and I…" Her hands landed on her flat tummy as if beckoned there. "I already love it. The baby."

Cheryl put another scoop of salad on her plate, then looked up at Brittany and grinned. "Rory's a great guy. I bet he'll be thrilled."

"You think?"

"He's crazy about you. He's wicked clannish. Why wouldn't he be crazy about a baby?"

Brittany smiled back at her friend and nodded, but her unease lingered, making the day crawl by like molasses. More than anything, she needed to see Rory's face and tell him what was going on. She hadn't meant for this to happen, of course, but it had, and they were both responsible.

As she made the bed in her little apartment after sending some donor-request e-mails on behalf of A Better Tomorrow, it suddenly occurred to her that when she'd least expected it, all of her dreams had suddenly come true: she had a family of friends at Summerhaven, she had true love with Rory, and now, she'd have a baby—the family she'd always longed for…if only Rory wanted it as much as she did.

As day turned to dusk, she took a drive into town and

bought a pregnancy test, split between the swelling of pure joy when the test turned positive and her impatience to share the news with Rory. The minutes ticked by. Five o'clock. Six o'clock. Finally, at seven o'clock, she heard the downstairs door open and slam shut and the sound of his shoes on the stairs.

She took a deep breath and braced herself, determined not to act weird or blurt out her news, no matter how much her secret begged to be told.

"Britt?" he called.

"Up here!"

He rounded the corner of the stairs into the loft, wearing a suit and tie, the smile on his face so wide, she was practically blinded by it.

A suit? Now, why was Rory wearing a suit?

"Where have you been?" she asked breathlessly, hurling herself into his open arms. "What happened?"

"Something great," he said, kissing her soundly before pulling away. He pulled one of two chairs from the tiny kitchen table. "Here. Sit down. I'll tell you everything."

She gulped, pushing her own news to the back burner as much as she could to concentrate on his. "Okay."

Once she was seated, he started. "In college, I had this idea. Conference centers like Summerhaven."

"And you did it," said Brittany. "You did a great job transitioning Summerhaven from a kids' camp to conference center."

"Thanks. Yeah. I did it here. But that's not where my idea ended. I wanted to open more than one. One here, outside of Boston. But another outside of Manhattan, and another near Raleigh. Another close to DC. You get it: a collection of camp-style, rustic but luxurious conference and event centers that businesses could use for retreats and team building but that were also available for weddings or—or anniversary parties…"

Brittany nodded, recalling the day Mrs. Toffle had shared Rory's idea with her. And Brittany had decided, a long time ago, that if he came to her and shared her idea, she'd offer to be his first investor. She didn't fear that Rory was only with her for her fortune or connections; she knew him far better than that. And she'd be happy to make his dreams come true, just as he had done for her.

"Sounds amazing," she said. "And I'd like to be—"

"I got it!" he cried, falling to his knees at her feet. "I got the money to do it! I have investors!"

"What? What do you mean?"

"I met with Colgate Venture Capital today. And they agreed to fund me. I have 1.3 million dollars to acquire property outside of Raleigh!"

"Rory!" she exclaimed, reaching for his beaming face and cupping it with her hands. "That's where you were today? That's what you were doing? You could have told me!"

His expression sobered a little as he shook his head. "I couldn't do that, Britt. I remember what you told me when we met that some men chased after you for your money, and I would never, ever want you—*even for a second*—to wonder if I had pursued you for a leg up. I needed to have the funding in place before I told you. I need to have something to share with you before I…"

His eyes—wildly intense—looked into hers, searching them.

"Before what?" she asked, sliding her hands from his face and clasping them in her lap.

He reached into his breast pocket and pulled out a small black box, his breath hitching as he held it out to her and snapped it open to reveal a diamond ring.

"Before asking you to be my wife."

She gasped in surprise, tears filling her eyes as she looked down at the small solitaire, which was much smaller than the previous engagement rings she'd received, yet infinitely more perfect for her in every way because of the man who offered it. "Oh, Rory…"

"I wanted to be able to provide for you. I mean, I know you'll always have your own money, and that's fine. But it was important to me…to have this. For us."

She clenched her jaw, trying to keep the tears from falling. This man—this strong, true, smart, beautiful man— had covered every base, placed her and her feelings above everything else in his life, and she was so overwhelmed with love and gratitude, she didn't think she could speak.

He plucked the ring from its white velvet bed and took her shaking hand in his. "Brittany Manion, I love you. I remember who you were as a teenager, but I fell in love with the woman you became. Please make me the happiest man on earth and say you'll marry me."

She inhaled sharply as tears coursed down her cheeks.

Of course she wanted to marry Rory Haven and live happily ever after. But she couldn't say yes. Not until he knew exactly what he was getting into.

She took a deep, shuddering breath. "R-Rory."

His eyebrows furrowed and his face fell, his breathing audible as he sucked in a breath and held it. He was worried, and she hated that—that she'd stolen his thunder by putting on the brakes for a minute—but she needed to share her news with him before the ring went on her finger. The lasting lesson of her disastrous relationship with Ben was the value of total transparency with her partner. She lifted her chin, grasping for the courage to be forthright and honest and tell Rory about her pregnancy *before* accepting his proposal.

"Rory, remember when we first met? Again, I mean? When I first came back here in the spring?"

He nodded, his eyes wide and worried, his frozen hand still holding up the ring between them.

"And I asked you…" She gulped. "I asked you if you—if, um, if you wanted kids."

His forehead wrinkled as he nodded slowly, still staring at her with that intense, uncertain expression.

"And you said"—she paused, taking a shaking breath before continuing—"um, you said that you were Irish and—and it was one of your specialties."

"Yeah," he said. "I remember. But what does that have to do with—"

"You may be even better at it than you thought."

Closing her mouth, she licked her lips nervously, then reached for the hand holding the ring and drew it to her abdomen, covering his hand, and the ring, with her palm.

"We're a package deal," she managed as Rory's bent head remained focused on their hands. "Me…and…and our…"

He was staring at her belly, but suddenly his head whipped up. His eyes slammed into hers, scanning them, his breathing faster and faster as a smile bloomed on his face—

small at first, then bigger and bigger until it was spread ear to ear. "Britt...*mo, mhuirnín*...are you saying what I think you're saying?"

She nodded quickly, her words spilling out. "We're going to have a baby, Rory. In May."

"Brittany!" he cried, standing up, then reaching down to pull her into his arms. He lifted her off the ground, spinning her around and around in the tiny room. "A baby! We made a baby!"

Laughing and crying at the same time, she held on for dear life and let him celebrate, all of her worries fading away as her husband-to-be reassured her that he was just as delighted about starting a family as she.

"I know the timing isn't perfect," she whispered breathlessly near his ear.

He stopped twirling her and leaned back, gazing into her brown eyes. "There could never be a bad time for news like this."

"I love you," she murmured, the words spilling from her lips with so much gratitude and awe, she could barely believe the sheer magnitude of her own happiness.

"I love you too." Holding her cheeks tenderly, he asked, "Is that a yes?"

She nodded, holding out her left hand so he could slip the ring on her fourth finger. "That's definitely a yes."

And as he bent his head to hers, capturing her lips in a sweet kiss, Brittany realized that Rory Haven—her teen crush, her true love, her fiancé, and the father of her lucky little baby—would also be her safe haven...forever.

THE END

TURN THE PAGE FOR A SNEAK PEEK AT…

(Tierney and Burr's story)

CHAPTER ONE

Bang. Bang. Bang.

Tierney Haven opened her eyes slowly, rolling to her side to look at the digital clock on her bedside table, but it was as dark as the rest of her room. Reaching over, she tapped the clock with her fingers, but nothing happened.

Thunder cracked and rumbled outside, and lightning split the sky in jagged white streaks, brightening her room.

Power must have gone out.

"Anyone home? Wake up!"

Bang. Bang. Bang.

It took her a moment to realize the banging that woke her wasn't thunder; it was coming from downstairs. Someone was knocking on her front door, yelling for her to wake up.

"Ian?" she mumbled, rubbing her bleary eyes and sitting up in bed as a fist slammed into the downstairs door again.

"Open up!" yelled the voice, growly with impatience and unmistakably male.

"*Damnú,*" she sighed in her mother's native Gaelic, swinging her legs over the side of the bed as more lightning lit her room with a brief phosphorescent strike. She plucked her glasses from the bed side table and put them on. The last time someone had pounded on Tierney Haven's door at two o'clock in the morning, it was her brother Ian on a bender. He'd show up out of the blue, after several months of living on the streets of Boston, and scared her to death.

"Why, Ian?" she muttered as a dark heaviness filled her heart. "You were doing so well!"

Bang. Bang. Bang.

She slipped her feet into waiting slippers and padded from the side of her bed to her bedroom door, making her way down the dark upstairs hallway to the stairs.

"I'm coming, Ian, you *diabhal*!" she said, reaching for the railing.

Four and a half months of sobriety down the drain, she thought, blinking back tears with every step she took. Four and a half months of Tierney and their brother, Rory, shepherding Ian to AA meetings and supporting his recovery. Four and a half months of hoping—every day— that Ian was closer to lifelong recovery. Four and a half months that made a person believe that four and a half months could turn into forever.

She swiped at her useless tears and lifted her chin as she reached the tiny landing, turned, then continued downward. Crying wouldn't help Ian. She needed to be strong now.

He'd likely rage around her cottage for a while, drinking whatever he had with him, before breaking down in tears and finally passing out. At that point, Tierney would need to pour any remaining alcohol down the sink and hide his keys and phone. The vomiting would begin when he woke up and last for a day or two. She'd eventually need to call Rory to come and help. But not yet. She could handle things until morning, and then maybe Rory could come over for a few hours before his camp day began.

Maybe she could get one of the docent interns to lead tours of the museum today. She hoped so, because Rory would have to get back to Summerhaven by breakfast, which meant Tierney would be back on "Ian duty" until tonight when Rory could come back and relieve her for a few hours.

"What a fucking mess," she muttered, stepping into her tiny living room, the hulking body of her drunk brother silhouetted by another slash of lightning in the stained-glass window on her front door. "*Cic maith sa tóin atá de dlíth air.*"

You need a good kick up the arse.

"*Damnú air! Oscail an doras!*" he yelled back. *Damn it! Open the door!*

Oh, great. His bloody Irish was top-notch tonight…which meant he was *beyond* shit-faced, because his Gaelic was always best when he was on a bender. She took a deep breath, then unlocked and unbolted the door, turning the knob and pulling open the heavy Spanish-style antique door so that Ian could fall inside.

With no outdoor light overhead, she could barely see the man in front of her, but when another bolt of lightning rent the sky, the first thing she noticed was that he had no hair. *A buzz cut.* And the second thing she noticed was that his unbuttoned shirt flapped open in the wind to reveal a chest covered tattoos, including one that ran from shoulder to shoulder and read, "Destroyer."

Ian has long hair, her horrified psyche whispered, *and no tattoos.*

A hand landed on her upper chest, pushing her back with such force that she was knocked off her feet and flew backward about five feet before landing on her ass. The stranger stepped into her living room and kicked the door shut behind him, turning briefly to bolt the door before facing her.

Thunder rumbled, and a moment later, multiple strikes of lightning through her windows lit up the man standing against the door. Tall and thickly muscled, he had no hair, a torso covered in ink, the butt of a gun peeking out from the waistband of his soaked jeans, and bare feet.

"Where are you?" he demanded, whipping his head right, then left.

Pitch darkness settled on the room again, the wind howling outside and the rain beating on the terra-cotta roof of the old caretaker's cottage.

Tierney, still sitting on the floor where she'd fallen, frozen with fear, stayed silent.

"Where...*the fuck*...are you?" he yelled breathlessly into the black room.

Did he realize that she'd fallen when he pushed her? She drew her legs to her chest, making herself as small as possible.

"I know...you're here!" he bellowed, his voice breathless and his speech stilted. "You opened...the fucking door!"

Scooting back as quietly as she could, Tierney's back touched her bookcase, and she slid slightly to the left, into the corner created by the bookcase and stairs. Meanwhile, she heard the stranger, who must have pulled his gun from his waistband, cock the hammer back.

"*Aiteann.*"

He growled the word, his voice low and furious.

4

Tierney sucked in a breath, shivering. *Aiteann* was the most vulgar of all Irish curse words, and although she'd heard it once or twice before during summer trips to Ireland with her family, it had never been directed at her.

Thunder blasted outside again, and Tierney wrapped her arms around her legs and bent her head, curling into a ball and staying as still as possible. Maybe he wouldn't see her when the lightning followed a second from now and lit up the room.He

As she huddled in the corner, waiting for the inevitable flash of light, a million terrible scenarios flooded her mind. Murder. Rape. Assault. Kidnapping. But what made her heart clench with desperation was the thought of never seeing her brothers again, of never hearing her father's voice or smelling her mother's perfume, Inis, ever again. Had she been a good enough sister? A faithful and loving daughter? Did they all know how much she loved them?

The lightning cracked, tearing open the sky and illuminating her cottage.

"There you are!"

A hand landed on her head, the fingers tangling in her hair and yanking hard. She cried out in pain, her knees scraping on the brick floor as he dragged her into the middle of the room, shoving her against the side of the couch before releasing her.

"Don't you dare…scream."

Scream? What was the point? She lived alone on thousands of acres of state land with no neighbors for miles. Even if she did scream, no one would hear. Her heart thundered in her ears, and her eyes burned with tears, but she bit the insides of her cheeks, refusing to cry, refusing to give him the satisfaction of a single sob.

Though it was dark as coal all around her, she could tell that he was squatting down in front of her. She could hear him breathing, shallow and loud, the whistle of a wheeze as he exhaled.

"Where's…the phone?" he demanded.

Her breath caught in her throat, making it impossible to answer.

"Where…is it?" he yelled at close range.

Speak, Tierney, speak!

"It's…I mean, um…"

"Where is the…the *fucking* phone?" he growled, his warm spittle landing on her cheeks.

She only had one phone, and it was charging upstairs on her bureau. She'd never had the little cottage wired for a landline.

"I don't have a…I mean—" She stopped speaking when she felt cold, hard metal slide against her temple.

"I am going…to shoot you…*in the fucking head*…if you don't tell me…where the phone is," he said, the words faster and angrier as they flew from his lips.

"*Éist liom!*" she begged in Irish. *Listen to me!*

Whether she saw a shadow of movement or just felt it, she wasn't certain, but there was a thread of surprise in his voice when he answered her in Irish:

"*Labhair.*" *Speak.*

"My—my phone is u-upstairs. On m-my bureau."

He lowered the gun from her face. "Stand up. We'll go…get it."

Gulping softly, Tierney braced her hand on the couch and stood up. He reached out in the darkness, grazing her breast through her nightgown before sliding his hand to her arm. Gripping it tightly, he said, "Lead the…way."

After living in the same place for five years, Tierney could walk about her cottage blindfolded, so it was easy for her to find the stairs and start climbing. But was it a mistake to lead him to her bedroom? Should she be fighting him off down here? What could she do? *What can I do?* Could she push him down the stairs? Sure, but maybe his gun would go off. *No, don't push him. Fight later, when you don't have a gun at your back.*

As they rounded the landing, she suddenly remembered an article she'd read about kidnapping victims. It advised if you were ever in a hostage situation, you should try to humanize yourself to your captor. It made them more likely to spare your life.

"You're…" She paused, trying to calm her erratic breathing and figure out a way to connect with him. "You're Irish."

"Shut up," he grunted, and for the first time, Tierney heard something else in his voice. It wasn't a feeling or an emotion. It was…*pain*. Raw pain. Real pain. Physical pain. He was in pain. That's probably why his speech was so breathless and stilted.

"*An bhfuil tú ceart go leor?*" she asked, trying to keep her voice gentle. *Are you okay?*

"I told you…to shut…the fuck up. K-Keep walking," he panted, shoving her forward as they reached the top of the stairs.

In the close space, she lurched forward and hit her forehead on the closed bathroom door in front of her. She gasped with pain. "Ow!"

"F-Fuck," he growled. "I didn't—sorry." Then, "Which w-way?"

Did he just apologize to me?

The question flashed through her brain, then disappeared just as quickly.

"Left or…r-right?"

"Left."

He yanked her arm to the left, walking down the short hallway to the open door of her bedroom.

"Where's"—his breathing was growing shallower by the minute, and if she wasn't mistaken, the grip on her arm was weakening—"the bureau?"

"Just there," she said.

His fingers on her arm were starting to shake. "W-Where?"

"Umm…" If she continued to stall, would she eventually be able to overpower him? To run away from him? "Over there. To your right."

He tried to pull her right, but his fingers slipped from her arm just as another bolt of lightning lit up the room. Tierney turned to face him, staring into his glassy, ice-blue eyes. Her gaze slid up to his forehead, which was covered with beads of sweat. *Fever*, she thought. *A bad one.*

Without thinking, she reached up with her free hand and laid it on his forehead, wincing at the scorching heat there. "You're burning up."

"Stop…arsing around," he said, jerking away, his breathing shivery and uneven. "Get the…f-fucking ph-phone."

He staggered forward, pushing her against the bedside table to the right of the bed, which crashed to the ground.

"Please, Mr...."

"*Brrr.*" He shivered, his body swaying before he fell backward onto her bed.

She slid away from him, keeping her back to the wall as she inched to the corner of the room, reaching for the phone on the edge of the bureau. She pulled it from the wall, cord and all, running her finger over the home button on the bottom and glancing at it as it came to life. *4:30 am.* A light-blue glow filled the room.

"I'm calling the police."

"No!" he screamed. "N-No police!"

Something in his tone—desperation, terror, maybe both—made her pause and look up. He wasn't exactly sitting up, but he was trying to.

"Why not?" she asked.

"P-Please."

"You need an ambulance."

"*Uihm p-póilíní,*" he groaned, his eyes at half-mast, his neck barely able to hold up his head. *No police.*

That's when Tierney saw the gun. Still held in his shaking hand, he raised it, pointing it at her.

"It's okay. No police," she said, holding up her hands and leaning back against the bureau. "Could you put the gun down?"

"No," he panted, shaking his head.

Tierney lowered her arms, glancing at the home screen on her phone and trying to remember the trick for calling 911 without dialing. But that's when she noticed something dire: she had no signal.

Her phone, which usually had at least two bars, had none.

She glanced out the window and realized that the house on the hill was just as dark as her cottage. Lightning must have hit the cell phone tower hidden in the barn by the main house. It had happened more than once before.

Shit. Fuck.

No. Don't panic.

Think, Tierney. Think.

She glanced at the bed, where the stranger still held a shaking gun trained on her, though she could see he was fighting to keep his eyes open. He was in bad shape and worsening by the moment.

"I won't call the police. I promise. Listen," she said gently, taking a step toward him, "you're obviously in trouble, but I don't want to hurt you. Put the gun down and you can have my phone, okay?"

"Give it," he said, holding out his other hand, which shook as badly as the first.

"There's no signal," she said, scrunching her shoulders up around her ears as she handed it to him and he grabbed it.

Clutching the phone in one hand and the gun in the other, he lay back on the bed, muttering, "I c-can't…d-die here."

With the phone resting on his bare chest, the blue glow illuminating his skin, Tierney noticed something else, something unusual and unexpected: a medal of Saint Michael lying on top of his tattoo.

"Saint Michael," she murmured. The warrior angel. The patron saint of policemen. Huh. Why would *this* man be wearing such a thing?

"Ssssaint…Miiiiiiiichael," he breathed. "If he c-could…k-kill the d-devil…so c-can I."

"Mr.…."

"Burrrrrr," he said again, and this time Tierney realized that he wasn't cold; he was telling her his name.

"Mr. Burr—"

"J-Just…Burrrrrr," he said, his eyes closed, his hands on his chest, still tightly clenched around his gun and her phone.

The adrenaline that had been pumping through her body had exhausted her, and as she realized that he was almost completely incapacitated, she relaxed a little, slumping against her bureau.

With two brothers her age, Tierney Haven had more than a little bit of experience reading men, but this one was throwing her for a loop. A Saint Michael medal sitting on top of a tattoo that read "Destroyer." Contradictions abounded.

Although he'd forced his way into her home, and his language and manner were rough, she didn't believe he'd come here to hurt her. In fact, since the moment he'd arrived, he'd been dogged in one pursuit: to use her phone.

Yes, he'd grabbed her hair to get her out of the corner of her living room, but he hadn't added a gratuitous slap or kick. Even when he'd touched her breast in an attempt to find her arm in the darkness, he hadn't lingered on it, hadn't copped an extra feel. And when he'd pushed her at the top of the stairs and she'd bumped her head, he'd *apologized* to her.

He's not here to hurt me, she decided, relaxing a little more. *But who was he? Where was he from? How did he get here? And why?*

His feet were still on the floor, though the rest of his

body was lying across her bed. She stepped to the edge of the mattress, leaning over him just a little.

"Burr?"

He groaned softly, his eyes fluttering open. "D-Don't g-go."

She gulped. His voice sounded so much like Ian's, she could almost close her eyes and believe he was her brother.

"Me?"

"You. D-Don't…want…to…d-die…alonnnnnne," he murmured, the last word drawn out like the word *amen* after the Our Father.

It did something to her heart, that terrible and simple request, and she cocked her head to the side, watching as he remained motionless on her bed.

After several minutes, she whispered his name again.

"Burr?"

He murmured in his sleep, groaning softly, but didn't open his eyes.

She sucked her bottom lip between her teeth as the screen on her phone went dark. The rain was finally letting up a little, and a faint lavender glow—a mix of moonlight and dawn—filtered into the room.

What do I do? What do I do now?

She backed away from the bed, looking out the window, and that's when she noticed his car. A little way down the road, outside the gate, the headlights and interior lights were on because the driver's-side door had been left open.

I should move his car, she thought, taking a concerned look at him before slipping quietly from the room.

She headed downstairs, grabbing an umbrella from the

antique bucket beside the front door, and headed out into the rain, grateful that the storm had subsided. It only took a few minutes to reach the gate and punch in the entry code. Luckily the gates opened inward, because his car would have been in the way had they opened outward.

It wasn't a fancy car—a blue Honda Accord—it was your run-of-the-mill city vehicle. Where was he from? Concord? No. Even in Concord, you'd need four-wheel drive to get anywhere from October to March. Hmm. Maybe Boston? Boston was the biggest big city within a couple hours' drive.

Peeking into the car, the first thing she noticed was a blackish stain on the driver's seat where his shoulder would have rested. Oil? She leaned closer, pressing her finger against the moisture and drawing it away. It was dark red on the pads of her fingers. Blood? She didn't remember seeing blood on his chest or arm, but there'd barely been enough light to get a good look at him, and frankly, an injury would explain his speech and fever.

She slid into the car, leaning forward so she wouldn't touch the upholstery with her white nightgown. Too far back for her to reach the pedals, she adjusted the seat forward, then pulled the door closed, driving through the gate and up the road to her cottage. Pulling the car into her driveway, she shifted it into park and turned on the interior lights. A pink bubblegum air freshener hung from the rearview mirror and an empty orange juice bottle sat in the center console. There was an open pack of wet wipes on the passenger seat, with several stained wipes littering the floor.

She opened the glove compartment, searching for clues about who he was, and found a sippy cup, two sparkly hair bands, ketchup packets, tissues, and the car's registration. The car was owned by someone named Suzanne Riley, whose address was listed as Dorchester, MA, a neighborhood located just south of Boston proper. Turning to look in the backseat, she found a booster seat that had a cup of Cheerios in the built-in cupholder and a stuffed bunny beside it on the seat.

Who was this Suzanne? Someone's mother, obviously. But who was she to Burr? Wife? Girlfriend? Or was the car stolen? Maybe he had no connection to Suzanne at all. Had he hurt the mother and child taking their car? Whose blood was on the driver's seat upholstery? She let the question sit for a moment, waiting for a feeling of dread to overwhelm her, but it didn't. She didn't know Burr at all, but something—intuition, surely—told her that he wasn't a murderer. If he was, she'd already be dead.

With far more questions than answers, she closed the glove compartment and withdrew the keys from the ignition. About to go back inside, her eyes flicked to the rearview mirror, landing on the trunk. *Hmmm.* Scooting from the driver's seat and rounding the car, she unlocked the trunk and looked inside. She found a half-opened black nylon duffel bag, which she hoisted onto her shoulder, and a brown Stop and Shop bag. Opening the paper sack, she looked inside to find neat stacks of money filling the lower fourth of the bag.

It had to be thousands of dollars.

Why would he be driving around with that? What was he into? Drugs? Weapons? Was he a gang member? And how did he end up outside her door tonight?

Shoving the paper bag back into the corner of the

truck, she slammed it shut and headed back into her cottage, closing the front door behind her. Motionless in the dark living room, she listened for a sound from upstairs, but heard nothing. With his duffel bag still on her shoulder, Tierney made her way to the kitchen and grabbed a flashlight, matches, and two candles from under the kitchen sink.

She placed the candles on the coffee table and lit them, then sat down on the couch with his bag beside her. Curious to know what was inside, she gulped before unzipping it the rest of the way and flicked on her flashlight.

On top she found a white T-shirt that was clean except for some bloody fingerprints, a pair of jeans, socks, and boxer shorts, and underneath the clothes—a pistol, a box of ammunition, a knife, a small pair of binoculars, two Kind bars, a bottle of orange juice, and a pair of handcuffs.

Hmm.

Now her thoughts shifted to the other side of the equation.

Saint Michael, a second gun, and handcuffs.

A cop? Could he be a cop? But why would a Boston cop find himself banging on her door in Moultonborough, New Hampshire, at four thirty in the morning? And why did he have thousands of dollars in his trunk and look like a gangbanger?

"Suze! Suzy!"

The anguished cry came from her bedroom.

Tierney zipped his bag shut, stood up, and turned to the stairs, knowing she had an important decision to make…

She could either walk back out her front door, get in her car, and drive to the Moultonborough Police Station or go upstairs and check on her unexpected guest.

What surprised Tierney the most was that her choice was already made, even before she'd laid it out for herself.

Maybe it was the fact that tonight had been scary, yes, but also exciting when life for Tierney, in general, had become fairly routine.

Or maybe it was that she knew he was in trouble and she wanted to help. Tierney had two brothers she loved more than anything—one of whom had been in trouble many times—and maybe once or twice, someone else's sister had looked after Ian. Maybe this man, Burr, had a sister who loved him as much as Tierney loved Ian. Looked at in a cosmic context, this was her opportunity to pay back that kindness.

Or maybe it was as simple as her own damned curiosity. Was he a destroyer or protector? A villain or hero? Tierney loved reading mysteries more than anything, pouring over them night after night on her Kindle from the safety of her bed. But here was a real, live mystery on her doorstep. If she turned him into the police, she might never find out where he came from and how he ended up finding his way to her.

One thing was for certain: her choice had *nothing* to do with his ice-blue eyes, strong jaw, muscular chest, and low, growly voice. She absolutely, positively *refused* to be attracted to such a raw, brutish sort of man, and that was that.

Clutching the flashlight to her chest, she turned away from the door and started up the stairs.

Thank you for reading
FIGHTING IRISH, *The Summerhaven Trio #1*

For announcements about upcoming Haven family books,
be sure to sign up for Katy's newsletter at
http://eepurl.com/disKlD

ALSO BY KATY

THE SUMMERHAVEN TRIO

Fighting Irish
Smiling Irish
Loving Irish

THE BLUEBERRY LANE SERIES

THE ENGLISH BROTHERS
(Blueberry Lane Books #1–7)

Breaking Up with Barrett
Falling for Fitz
Anyone but Alex
Seduced by Stratton
Wild about Weston
Kiss Me Kate
Marrying Mr. English

THE WINSLOW BROTHERS
(Blueberry Lane Books #8–11)

Bidding on Brooks
Proposing to Preston
Crazy about Cameron

SMILING IRISH

Campaigning for Christopher

THE ROUSSEAUS
(Blueberry Lane Books #12–14)

Jonquils for Jax
Marry Me Mad
J.C. and the Bijoux Jolis

THE STORY SISTERS
(Blueberry Lane Books #15–17)

The Bohemian and the Businessman
The Director and Don Juan
Countdown to Midnight

<u>a m o d e r n f a i r y t a l e</u>
(A collection)

The Vixen and the Vet
Never Let You Go
Ginger's Heart
Dark Sexy Knight
Don't Speak
Shear Heaven

At First Sight
Coming 2018

Fragments of Ash
Coming 2018

19

Swan Song
Coming 2019

<u>STAND-ALONE BOOKS</u>

After We Break
(a stand-alone second-chance romance)

Frosted
(a romance novella for mature readers)

Unloved, a love story
(a stand-alone suspenseful romance)

about the author

New York Times and **USA Today** **bestselling author Katy Regnery** started her writing career by enrolling in a short story class in January 2012. One year later, she signed her first contract, and Katy's first novel was published in September 2013.

Thirty-five books later, Katy claims authorship of the multititled *New York Times* and *USA Today* bestselling Blueberry Lane Series, which follows the English, Winslow, Rousseau, Story, and Ambler families of Philadelphia; the six-book, bestselling ~a modern fairytale~ series; and several other stand-alone novels and novellas, including the critically acclaimed, *USA Today* bestselling contemporary romance *Unloved, a love story.*

Katy's first modern fairytale romance, *The Vixen and the Vet,* was nominated for a RITA® in 2015 and won the 2015 Kindle Book Award for romance. Katy's boxed set, *The English Brothers Boxed Set,* Books #1–4, hit the *USA Today* bestseller list in 2015, and her Christmas story, *Marrying Mr. English,* appeared on the list a week later. In May 2016, Katy's Blueberry Lane collection, *The Winslow Brothers Boxed Set,* Books #1–4, became a *New York Times* e-book bestseller.

Katy's books are available in English, French, German, Italian, Portuguese, and Turkish.

Katy lives in the relative wilds of northern Fairfield County, Connecticut, where her writing room looks out at the woods, and her husband, two young children, two dogs, and one Blue Tonkinese kitten create just enough cheerful chaos to remind her that the very best love stories begin at home.

Sign up for Katy's newsletter today: www.katyregnery.com!

Upcoming (2018) Projects

Smiling Irish, The Summerhaven Trio #2
Loving Irish, The Summerhaven Trio #3
At First Sight, a modern fairytale novella
Fragments of Ash, a modern fairytale

Connect with Katy

Katy LOVES connecting with her readers and answers every e-mail, message, tweet, and post personally! Connect with Katy!

9 781944 810276